Hello Navi

Cindy
Many Blessings!
Love,
Sandy
John 4:10

Hello Navi

a novella about human trafficking

Written by a Survivor, Based on Actual Events

SANDY STORM

ISBN-13: 9781945786006
ISBN-10: 1945786000

Dedication

to my husband, who has always loved me as Christ loves the church

Foreword

~

By Minta Moore

Founder, New Life Refuge Ministries

P.O. Box 9157

Corpus Christi, TX 78469

361.946.6331

NewLifeRefugeMinistries.org

*T*he Lord intersected my life with the author's in 2010, just as I was being stirred to start a home for survivors of sex trafficking. Our intersection was not because she had been a victim of sex trafficking but, rather, she herself was involved with an anti-trafficking organization. Someone had given me her name and phone number because they had seen her speak on the issue of domestic minor sex trafficking and thought we should talk. That was the beginning of a journey of friendship. Over the next few years our lives continued to cross sporadically as she left the anti-trafficking world to peruse other endeavors.

At the Lord's leading I called my friend to ask her to be a prayer partner and we started meeting weekly for coffee and prayer. It was during one of those morning meetings she shared with me that she had been a victim of domestic minor sex trafficking, which led to exploitation and sex trafficking as an adult, and she was saved when Jesus boldly intersected her life. As time when on, she shared bits and pieces of her story of being a victim. I was amazed at the work the Lord had done in her life and I continue to be amazed at what a true "beauty from ashes" story she represents. By all human accounts she should be the most bitter, dissociative, schizophrenic, resentful person alive. However, none of those words describe her at all. She is the most loving, caring, community involved and sound minded person I know, and she gives all the credit and glory to Jesus.

It was also during one of our morning meetings that my friend shared with me that the Lord was leading her to write a book about her story. A book that would help other victims see that there is hope and healing for them just like what she has received. Her vision for this book went beyond inspiring other survivors and included impacting people like you and I in a way that would dare to educate us on the realities of Domestic Minor Sex Trafficking. I was honored when she asked me to be the first person to read it. She would send me the chapters via email after she would get one completed. Over the next several months, I read the stories she recounted of her victimization and I stood in awe of her being a new creation, truly only what Jesus can do.

As you dive into the pages of <u>Hello Navi,</u> beware. This is not a sugar-coated story, but instead a tale of truly turning ashes into beauty. It will encourage those who feel there is no hope, and it will educate others on the grim reality of how this crime can happen all around us. We never know it is going on until our eyes are opened. I encourage you to share what you learn from this book and educate those in your circle of influence, because we must be vigilant in fighting this crime. After all, *"Education is the most powerful weapon which you can use to change the world,"* said the late Nelson Mandela.

I'm going to take advantage of having your attention and have a "soap box" moment to share some of the realities of domestic minor sex trafficking. This is defined in the Victims of Trafficking and Violence Protection Act of 2000 as "sex trafficking in which a commercial sex act is induced by force, fraud, or coercion, or in which the person induced to perform such act has not attained 18 years of age.... " Experts generally agree that the trafficking term applies to minors whether the child's actions were forced or appear to be voluntary.

Sex trafficking of minors is a supply and demand business. Traffickers are just "businessmen" supplying what is being demanded, which is sex with young girls and boys. I tell anyone that will listen that the root of this exploitation is pornography. Unless we deal with it at the root, we will forever have people willing to supply our future, which is our kids, to satisfy that demand.

You see, pornography creates the demand to purchase sex because *"For as he thinks within himself, so he is."* Proverbs 23:7 NASB. I actually have sympathy for the buyers, as most truly believe this is a "victimless" crime. However, once they know the realities of prostitution and sex trafficking they are often remorseful and rarely buy sex again. These statements are based on the recidivism rates of men who attend "John Schools."

Back to pornography; adult and child trafficking victims are often used to make the pornographic videos and movies. Pornography is also often used to train child victims what to do and it normalizes the things that will be happening to them when they are with a "john".

America's future is being molested away as we sit by and do nothing.

John Wesley said, *"What we tolerate today the next generation will embrace."* We are in scary times if we can just sit back and not address this issue. It is only getting worse as it's all the while becoming more and more socially acceptable. We know things are getting out of control when there are TV shows that our kids watch with *"Pimp"* in the title and clothing lines that our kids wear with *"Hooker"* in the name. There are even pole dancing kits marketed to toddlers. We are part of the problem for not standing against this normalization of an over-sexualized culture. What are we thinking?

I quote one pimp who said "I don't have to train my girls, society does it for me." The next time your kids or grandkids sit down to watch television and you assume because it's targeted at children it's wholesome, I suggest you take a moment to see what the messages are in the show as well as what is being advertised. Remember, "… *the Devil walks about like a roaring lion, seeking whom he may devour."* 1 Peter 5:8 NKJV; and *"The thief (**The Devil**) does not come except to steal, and to kill, and to destroy (**our kids and our future**). I (**JESUS**) have come that they may have life, and that they may have it more abundantly."* John 10:10 NKJV, emphasis mine.

May God bless you and be with you through the journey you are about to take into the pages of <u>Hello Navi</u>, and may you be moved to action after reading this book.

Author's Note

~

I truly believe if the New Life Refuge Ministries "Home of Hope" had existed when I was a young victim of sex trafficking, I would have received the much needed care, counseling and healing from the trauma I endured. Instead of continuing for nearly 15 years in a cycle of drug abuse, depression, failed relationships and continued victimization by pimps, drug dealers and boyfriends, my story could have been quite different. The care and support of a committed group of therapists and counselors may very well have been exactly what I needed to break the cycle and find freedom from the shame and stigma of the abuse and exploitation I had undergone.

Human trafficking is the second largest and fastest growing criminal enterprise in the world, and there are an estimated 27 million people – of which 13 million are children – trapped in slavery at this moment. Trafficked persons often suffer torture tactics including sexual abuse, imprisonment, and starvation. The increasing demand for sex services provides a lucrative business for organized crime units, as well as individual perpetrators. This ever growing enterprise is continuously growing due to the relatively low risk of punishment, high profit returns, and a "commodity" that is reusable. According to the FBI and Center for Missing and Exploited Children, 100,000-300,000 American children are at risk of being trafficked each year. Currently there are less than 300 beds for those rescued.

New Life Refuge Ministries is working to be part of the solution to this growing problem and the work Minta Moore and her team are doing is vital to bringing an end to domestic minor sex trafficking. They are bringing awareness through education to recognize and prevent domestic minor sex trafficking, building a refuge of healing for the young survivors and they have been faithful to partner with other organizations to help sex trafficking survivors. They have also created a collaborative effort among governmental and non-governmental agencies to build a victim-centered approach to care for those who survive this horrific crime.

Not only are they a non-profit 501(c)(3) corporation, but I have watched them from the inception and can say with confidence they have proven to be good stewards of all they have been entrusted with. If, after reading this book, you feel compelled to do something to fight the atrocity of domestic minor sex trafficking, please consider making a tax-deductible contribution to their ministry, host a Party with a Purpose, or consider joining their prayer network. Please visit their website NewLifeRefugeMinistries.org to learn more about their efforts and how you can get involved.

You can also learn more about ways to recognize and identify victims, get educated on myths and misconceptions about trafficking and learn how you can report a tip or request services for a victim at the National Human Trafficking Resource Center's website, TraffickingResourceCenter.org. Keep their toll free tip line phone number programmed in your cell phone so you can call in a tip when you see suspicious activity; 1-888-373-7888.

Table of Contents

Is this the life You have chosen for me?

Is this real?

or is this a dream?

Why can't I just let You be

and totally

let go of me?

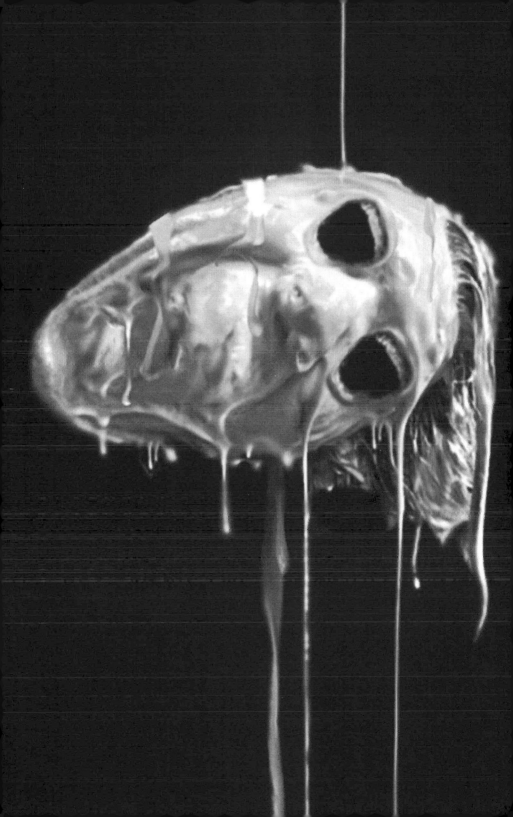

One

~

"Stems and Stones May Break My Bones, But It's My Own Thoughts That Destroy Me"

Navi sat on the edge of the bed and closed her eyes, trying to recall. She squinted intently, furrowing her brow and clenching her teeth, the little wrinkles on her forehead folding up on top of one another as she held her breath, diving deep into her mind and imagining sifting through a card catalogue of snapshot-like memories.

Aha! Here was one, she could see him standing in his blue pea-coat along the water in Paris. He had that crooked little smile that caused his eyes to twinkle just enough that anyone just glancing his way would be sure to tell he was giddy with excitement.

"No, wait," she thought, "that's just a photo from when he was in the service that I found last summer in an old box. He must have sent it home for someone to show me, but I definitely wasn't there. I've never been to Paris!"

Turning inward again, she searched and searched. "Where was that file? Surely there is one memory of my father somewhere in my brain!" she thought as she continued to grow more exasperated. She pulled up another image, this time of her on his lap. She was smiling so big and holding her soft little puppy named Rags. She must have been about 2 years old and had just had her bangs trimmed straight across, right above her tiny eyebrows, and her father stared at the camera with that same crooked smile. Frustrated again, she realized this was just another photo she had been shown when she was in kindergarten when she came home asking questions after her class had Dad's Day.

Back then she had been told that her dad was sick and had to go away, but a few years later she learned that he had been strung out on drugs and he had taken his own life when she was three years old.

Navi thought that maybe the meditation chanting she had read about would work. She closed her eyes and started repeating in her mind, "Father. Father. Father...." Laying herself back on the greasy, stiff, flowered hotel comforter she kept chanting, eyes closed and nose pointed up at the stained ceiling. "Father, father, father, father..." she was whispering now, barely audible, but there was no one else in the tiny dive of a motel room to hear her anyway.

"Fatherfatherfatherfatherfather..." now fully verbalizing and speaking aloud, she started chanting the word over and over and meditating. She opened her eyes and saw an image hovering above her of a large man on top of her who had his head turned slightly, his teeth and eyes clenched in ecstasy.

"NO!" she shouted loudly and as she threw her eyes open the image disappeared. She sat straight up and reached to the nightstand. Grabbing her glass pipe and twirling it in her shaking hands, she started fumbling in the drawer, searching for her stash.

She was almost afraid to look in the dark drawer because she had spotted some 3 and 4 inch long cockroaches crawling around in the bathroom when she first came into the room. Her hand felt the little baggie in the corner of the drawer and she sat it on top of the stand. Dumping out a few big shiny white rocks with her right hand, she held the pipe in her left hand, scooped them up and packed them into the burnt end.

"He wasn't really my father," she said to herself. "He just told me he was. I remember him always saying, 'Only

3

daddies get to love their little girls with this special secret love.'" Again she turned her nose up towards that dirty, stained ceiling, but this time she held the pipe up in one hand and, placing it to her lips, she took the blue flame of the lighter in her other hand and touched the glistening rocks, causing them to sizzle and melt into the burnt brillo pad she had pushed inside of the glass to act as a filter.

As the dope melted and started soaking into the brillo, a thick plume of smoke began to form near where she held the lighter. She lowered the glass stick parallel with the floor and inhaled, causing the smoke to shoot down the pipe and into her lungs. She twisted and twirled the pipe and ran the flame all around the tip, inhaling slowly and deeply so she could take in all the smoke. She felt her lungs expanding to hold it all as she kept burning the end and sucking in deeper until the lighter burned her thumb. She let go and threw the hot lighter against the wall but kept twisting the pipe and sucking in the thick smoke until no more came through. Then, slowly taking the pipe from her lips, she leaned back on the bed, holding in the smoke as she let herself fall into the all-to-familiar never ending hole. Going back in slow motion but at the speed of light, she let herself be taken up and carried into that dream-like place where only the first hit can take you.

Her ears were ringing and her skin turned clammy as little sweat beads started breaking out above her brow. She had laid completely back on the filthy motel comforter and let her arms and legs melt into oblivion, all the time holding her pipe just so, in order to keep the sticky oils she had melted into it from dripping out. Pursing her lips, Navi blew out the smoke through the greasy little circle she had formed with her lips, slowly at first, but then opening her mouth wide like a cat yawning and letting the cloud pour out. She felt her lungs deflate as she exhaled and opened her eyes to see the room literally filled with the thick, pungent haze.

"Oh yessss, now that's so much better," she mumbled, the corners of her mouth turning up into a dopey smile. "Now I can't even remember what I was trying to forget."

Her body seemed to be melting into the bed while her heart was set to pumping a deep dum-da-dum-da-dum. She could feel the atmosphere, the very air around her, pressing against every part of her body and making her feel both heavy and weightless at the same time as she hovered in a state of limbo between nearly comatose and full speed ahead.

The high only lasted a few minutes and then the sharp reality of the dingy room started to set in again. Pushing herself up onto her elbows, she groped the top of the nightstand for another glistening slab and, cramming it in the top of her stem she took her spare lighter from the nightstand. Navi was always trying to get one step ahead of the drug, and she desperately wanted to get this hit before the first one wore off. Raising her pipe, she put her lips around the tip and fired away, lowering the pipe and twisting and spinning it while melting the rock as it turned to oil. She was taking in all she could of the $20 hit she had loaded into the glass and again her ears rang, but not like the hit ten minutes before. This time when she exhaled she formed a circle with her lips and sent little rings floating around the room. She got the rush and the taste and the warmth and the chills again, but in the back of her mind she was realizing that she needed to ration this dope if it was going to last her all night.

She let herself recline back on her elbows and started thinking ahead. There was $5.17 and a few random items in the little backpack by her feet and that was really all she had to her name. The money she had used for this dope and the room had come from panhandling in front of a little store on the corner, and what she really wanted to use the money for was to get on a bus and ride back to her hometown to get clean and straightened up.

What Navi didn't know, however, was that this dope had a tighter grip on her than what she had been using in the past. This wasn't just crack or freebase cocaine, this mix of cocaine and heroin was different and much more powerful.

When she had first arrived in Memphis, she immediately went into some very dark places looking to turn off her brain. The drug addicts and street people she had hooked up with weren't just smoking coke; all the dope that was going around was a super powerful mix of cocaine and heroin, and she was hooked badly. She would get dope-sick if she went longer than five or six hours without a hit and the desperation was almost deadly once it started setting in. This stuff had such a tight grip on her she had to constantly stay a step ahead of running out. The last thing she wanted was to have to think about rationing her stash this early in the night but, she knew she was going to need to stretch it as long as she could. That chump change in her pocket wasn't gonna do anything for her tomorrow.

Laying back on that dirty bed, Navi started considering trying to get out of this town and knew there was no denying that it would eventually be necessary for her to get away from this place she had ended up in. It seemed this whole city seethed with evil; there was such hopelessness and sinfulness and everyday she was getting closer and closer to the line she had always swore she wouldn't cross.

Remembering back to when she had only barely arrived, she thought about how easily she had found herself caught up in a circle of young, drug addicted thieves and prostitutes. These weren't just girls who hung out with guys who would buy them drugs all night and then end up in bed with them when all the dope ran out, these were street-walking, bringing guys to hotels that charge by the hour, pulling up their skirts for a quick $10 or $20 in an alley kind of prostitutes.

The group of thieves had taught her everything there was to know about breaking into cars in dark parking lots. Many a night she played the look-out while they would make their rounds stealing the cash boxes from soda machines. A Coke machine in a good spot could have a few hundred dollars in $1 bills smashed down in the little black box inside the flimsy plastic outer casing. Navi wondered why people who counted on the few dollars they could collect from selling cans of soda would use a cheap little dime store lock to protect their livelihood. Those cheap locks could get popped off with a butter knife and in three minutes or less the black box full of dollar bills could be removed. In no time, she and the crew would speed off down the road, headed to the dope man's house to score again. The dope boys were used to getting paid in one dollar bills and quarters, but when the cash had been crammed up for so long, it could take hours to flatten the money out and count it.

These were lows she had always promised herself she would never sink to. But she would justify every act, telling herself she was only the lookout and that because she didn't physically rob the car or take the money out of the machine she wasn't really stealing. Or that she was just in the room while the other girl turned the trick so she wasn't really selling herself. But, she knew all along she was lying to herself and these things were adding up to a bigger karmatic debt than she would ever be able to repay. She knew if there really was a God that she would never be able to be good enough to come to Him, that she had gone too far in the wrong direction for too long.

All kinds of thoughts started working themselves to the top of her mind. One by one they floated up and whispered to her consciousness and, with a clash, her numbed-out state collided with the realities of her situation: the little money she had soon running out, the girls turning their tricks in front of her, the boys jamming their butter knives into the soda machines, the man hovering over her with his eyes and teeth clenched in ecstasy.

That was the breaking point. She shot up like a rocket and reached her shaking hands out to pack her stem again. Another $20 rock stuffed in the end - lips, lighter, inhaling, holding it in, blowing it out...but this time the numbness was so much fainter, the echo of the memory, though stale, was still in her mind, creating that oh-so-familiar hopelessness and deep despair. This was the fourth or fifth hit and the insane feeling of frustration would always set in about now. She started to hear that whisper that told her there was no way to run from her own mind, nowhere to turn that would release her from the memories of all of the horrible things that she had done and the memories of things that had been done to her. Smoking dope and running away were the only coping mechanisms she had, and they both constantly failed her.

Melting backward onto the greasy hotel comforter and again falling into the deep inky blackness of despair, she began to allow herself to listen to that voice telling her there was no hope, no escape from the torturous realities of her pathetic life and, as a result, she was becoming completely despondent, depressed to the point that she wasn't even able to lift her head.

As if by invitation, a thick demonic presence started to slither its way up from the filthy torn carpet, wrapping around her feet and ankles, making its way up her legs, then between her legs, around her stomach, clenching slightly like a boa constrictor about to apply its massive, deadly pressure full force.

Navi was lying on her back horizontally across the tiny bed with her feet on the floor - torso sideways. As she stared at the stained ceiling with her eyes wide open, a fountain of tears started streaming down her cheeks. She wasn't sobbing or crying, she actually barely even felt the emotions that would normally trigger tears to flow like this, but still they were coming in buckets. Turning her head slightly, she caused the tears to run over the little dam made by her upper lip and they started to trickle into her mouth. She felt the warmth and the wetness but the tears didn't taste salty like she had expected they would.

She didn't realize it, but she was severely dehydrated and malnourished, her body sorely lacking many of the vitamins and minerals it needed to be healthy and function properly. If she had really thought about it, she would remember that she hadn't eaten in days and the last thing she drank was part of a lukewarm 40 ounce beer she shared with two dirty homeless men behind the convenience store on the corner earlier in the day.

Slowly sitting up, she used the back of her hand to smear the snot and tears from around her mouth and once again reached toward the now much smaller pile of flaky white chunks. She went to pack the end of her pipe again and the black slithery demon wrapped itself around her shoulder, then her arm and made its way quickly to her hand. She was reaching for another $20 hit, which was already twice as much as a man more than twice her size would smoke at one time. The dark spirit was now completely covering her hand and forcing her to put twice that much and then some more on the tip of the stem. It forced her back on the bed violently, manipulating her into bringing the pipe and the lighter up to her face.

The spirit had spread across her and was now covering her like an oozing second skin, taking over her arms and hands, stomach, legs and feet. Once she started to inhale the monstrous hit on the pipe, he went inside the glass, kissing her quivering lips as he passed and entering her lungs along with all the smoke. He was wrapping himself around her body, glazing her chest, her neck, her face with the oozy tar-like coating. Intently working to cover every inch of her outer body, he began releasing the ooze into her bloodstream. Going out from her lungs, he started ripping his way through the highways that her veins and arteries made inside of her, all the while covering her organs and guts with the thick blackness. He was pulsating on top of her, throbbing inside of her and becoming fully integrated with her every part. As she inhaled deeper and deeper, it seemed the hit she was taking was unending and her lungs were filling with so much smoke they were about to burst. All this time, the evil spirit was ravaging her, inside and out, having his way with her.

She was being squeezed now, the constrictions and contractions deep and painful and keeping her from moving on her own. All she could do was twist the pipe between her finger and thumb, sucking more and more of the smoke through her pursed lips while working the torch lighter in her other hand. The demon had nearly penetrated every part, and he had made himself known throughout her whole body, in almost every hidden crevice. He was diligently working now to enter and capture her heart. He kept forcing her to suck the end of that pipe while the oils ran down the sides of it, coating her lips and fingers. He wrapped around her fiercely beating heart and set himself intently on taking this most precious part of Navi for himself and his king. The darkness furiously striving to find an entry point to slither in through but couldn't find a passage. He frantically began to lose his grip on the rest of her body; becoming frustrated, he realized that this heart was off limits, even with the drugs still pouring into her body.

Just then, a huge crash was heard as a massive man kicked in the door to the room. The dark spirit seemed to all at once gather itself up, quickly vacating the inner parts as well as the surface of Navi's body. She sat straight up and screamed, thrusting the hot glass tube and lighter against the wall and busting them into a million pieces. The darkness hovered above her, its beady eyes fixed fast on the form standing at the threshold of the door. Thick, pungent smoke was pouring out of the now splintered doorway and Navi was horrified as she looked down and realized she was completely nude. She jumped up and pulled on the rumpled pair of jeans and wafer-thin tank top that were in a pile at the foot of the bed.

The huge man stepped in to occupy the space and with a great move of force and power, he swept his arm through the air and splattered the dark blob against the back wall of the room. The man's eyes were made of fire and they were glowing and changing to the colors of an electric rainbow. He bore his teeth and released a noise that sounded at once like both a deep roar and a loud trumpet blast. The sound alone caused the splattered dark stain to wince and grimace and shake and finally dissipate and scurry out of the room, leaving through the windowsill and the edge of the carpet where the floor met the wall, slithering away until it was completely gone.

Navi was beyond terrified and, with her heart nearly pounding out of her chest, she scooped up her little backpack and ran right past the giant of a man, out the door and into the bright blazing daylight of a Tuesday afternoon.

Two

~

"RUN!"

Navi ran!

She ran down the skinny sidewalk in front of the row of little motel rooms, passing by the broken down cars covered with dust from the parking lot.

She ran around the side of the old brick building, through the grass and up a little hill behind the room she had been occupying. A rickety metal fence separated her from a sea of trees and, without missing a beat, she scaled the fence and found herself in the woods.

She nimbly ran between the trees, feeling the cool mud squishing between her toes and splashing in shallow puddles that sprayed the back of her worn jeans with little droplets of brown water.

Heart pounding and red-faced, her breath was coming out in little puffs and she ran and ran and ran. She was truly terrified and could think of nothing but getting as far away from that motel as she could but, as long as her strides were, she couldn't go fast enough. As she ran through the little forest trying to think a step ahead, she considered climbing a tree, digging a hole, hiding under a pile of leaves...but she didn't stop, she RAN!

Flashing through her mind was the image of the black blob that had hovered over her like a cloud. She had no idea what that was and even though she had just witnessed it with her own eyes she wanted to doubt it was really real. And that huge man who had kicked the door into a thousand tiny splinters was too large to be a real human! He was the same size as the doorway, his shoulders actually were wider than the door frame and he must have ducked his head when he entered because the top of his head was skimming the ceiling! She remembered the flash of the blue uniform he wore, the badge on his chest, the large black gun in his hand!

"Oh my God! He was pointing that gun right in my face! He was going to shoot me!" Navi thought to herself frantically as she continued to run. With that memory pushing her forward she now had even more reason to flee. That humongous man was a police officer and he must have been there to arrest her, or shoot her or kidnap her or something! And she was certain he was chasing her now, him and his policeman colleagues and their police dogs. She could almost hear them sloshing through the mud behind her, their police dogs barking and yelping as they were hunting her down!

Navi ran even harder now, pumping her fists and expertly bobbing and weaving past low hanging branches and around the thick trees. She leaped over little patches of briers, running her bare feet along the thorns and scraping her legs and ankles. Little bloody scratches were appearing on her arms and hands and feet but she didn't slow down, she just kept running and running and running.

The harsh sunlight of the early autumn sky was being filtered through the tall leafy branches and as she ran her eyes were straining to focus ahead on where her next turn would be. Now that she had realized the police were chasing her she had a renewed motivation to keep moving forward and not look back. As she squinted ahead she thought she caught a glimpse of a man dressed in torn black clothing running in front of her in the same direction, but then the image vanished. She kept pressing forward, now looking ahead to see if there was in fact someone up there running as she was, trying to get away from that huge cop and his cop buddies and their cop dogs.

She saw it again, the figure of a man sprinting ahead of her, his black tattered clothes blowing behind him like kite tails as he ran. He was looking back and his face was covered in absolute terror. Navi assumed that meant that the men and dogs chasing them were getting closer so she sped up too, grunting and sweating as she pushed herself even harder to flee their grip. The man in the torn black clothes was staying ahead of her but she was quickly gaining on him. She ran like her life depended on it, and for all she knew it did. Her life and her freedom hung in the balance as she splashed through the muddy puddles.

The man in black had darted off to the right, around one exceptionally large old tree and Navi turned to follow when she got to the spot where she had last seen him. She kept running, now going down a steep grade and she could see much better now as the trees had cleared out quite a bit. She was stepping gingerly, trying to keep herself moving forward down the hill but at the same time maintaining her balance so she wouldn't tumble head over heels to the bottom. She couldn't see the man anymore and wondered how he had just disappeared into thin air.

As she came to the bottom of the hill, she heard her feet crunching in a bed of crispy leaves and she suddenly realized that all she could hear was that crunching of those leaves. Navi stopped short and stood as still as a statue with her head cocked to the side, listening intently for the sound of the canine patrol that she had been fleeing from. She held her breath and stretched her neck, concentrating to hear anything other than the pounding of her own heart that was filling her ears with its booming echoes. She heard the long, low whistle of one lone bird and a croak from a cricket or a toad and then she heard the sound of the wind whisking through the trees and turning up some of the leaves piled at her feet. She did not hear the men and dogs who had been pursuing her.

Looking frantically around, she saw she was now at the edge of the woods. There was a wall of daylight just beyond the little force field of elms she was hidden by and the pulsating sun was glimmering through the swaying branches at the perimeter of the grove of trees. She scanned the forest's meandering boundary, once again spotting the man in black. He was standing about 60 yards from her, right at the fringe of the woods, barely concealed from whoever may be on the other side. He was facing her and actually staring deeply at her, almost like he was beckoning her to himself. As she looked at him she shifted her weight and turned her body so she was lined up with his.

As quickly as he had appeared in front of her, he ducked his head a bit, turned and stepped out of the woods and into the open area just beyond the rim of Navi's little thicket. She gasped at the humorousness of his disappearing in an instant like that but she couldn't help but be intrigued to see where he had gone. She crouched down and made her way through the crunchy leaves at the edge of the trees, and with a deep breath she exited the woods in the precise spot she had seen her mystery man vanish.

Now that she was out in the wide open, Navi suddenly felt vulnerable. She remembered the group of law enforcement men and dogs she was being chased by and felt her stomach clench. She looked around and realized she was probably in a safer place standing here than she was running or hiding in the woods. From where she stood she could see a corner convenience store, a fire station, a small park containing a worn old shelter-house and a run-down jungle gym and next to it a low-income neighborhood filled with small brick houses, nearly every one with its own banged-up, rusty car parked in front of it.

She stood very still and considered her options. Going to the fire station for help was definitely out of the question, they would hand her over to that giant cop right away since they would probably be aligned with him. There was nowhere to hide at the park, and besides, a few young kids were playing on the merry-go-round. The thought of wandering through the convenience store was out, considering she was barefooted and covered with mud and bloody scrapes from her knees down. That left her with no choice but to trek through the neighborhood and hope not to draw too much attention to herself. Navi took a deep breath and stepped onto the dusty sidewalk and felt the cool concrete. Her feet had started to ache a little more with each passing moment since she had been standing at the edge of the path.

She made her way down the wobbly sidewalk, past the little boxy houses with their little boxy yards. There were bars and gates on most of the windows and doors and none of the homes had any kind of charm or decorations. They each seemed to be their own sad shade of reddish-gray brick with little concrete stoops and a set of three steps leading down to the dirty walkway. The yards were full of short brown and yellow-green clumps. It was probably grass in the spring but, with no water from the hose and little rain from the sky this summer, it had all but dried up and burnt away.

The only thing Navi could concentrate on was keeping her head down and moving forward on the path beneath her feet. There were some people out and about in the neighborhood but, much to her surprise, they didn't seem to take much notice of her in spite of her obviously disheveled appearance. She did feel the stares of a group of four or five young teenaged boys who were standing by a car on the opposite side of the street. They stopped their conversation as she walked by and followed her with their eyes. She had no idea what she would do or say if anyone spoke to her but she was prepared to take off like a bolt of lightning and run for her life again if they approached her. The further she made it down the block the less interested they were in watching her.

Navi took a right and at the end of the next block she hung another right, passing what seemed like endless rows of sad, dilapidated brick homes. Her feet were pounding against the cool concrete, left - right - left - right - left - right.

She kept her head down and fists clenched, on edge and a ball of nerves. At last she could see the end of the street and another opening.

At the corner was a different convenience store, an old primary school with each of the windows either broken or boarded up and a set of run-down brick apartment buildings enclosed by a rusty chain link fence. There seemed to be a lot of activity going on there with lots of cars coming and going with their windows down and music turned up. People were milling around in the parking lot, running down the flights of concrete stairs, bending over into the open car windows and then turning to run back up the stairs. Navi knew these were crack houses and she knew that she was about to start feeling the effects of the small amount of dope she still had in her system starting to wear off.

She decided to cross the parking lot of the little convenience store and make her way to the brick and concrete apartments. She was determined to find a way to get her fix. Just as Navi stepped out into the oil-stained lot a dark red Cadillac pulled right in front of her and stopped, separating her from the brick buildings she was headed for. The passenger window lowered and she could instantly smell the unmistakable odor of pot smoke coming from a skunk weed blunt.

She saw through the smoke a dark skinned man dressed in a silky purple shirt with a fedora hat perched on his forehead, sitting in the leather driver's seat with his left hand dangling across the steering wheel. "You don't wanna go over thar little gurrl," he said to her, his words coming out slowly with a thick southern drawl. "Them boys'll eat you up gurrl, you aint but a small little thing walkin out hurr all bare-footed. Get in mah cadillac car and I'll take you down the road a piece and get you all cleaned up gurrl, walking 'round hurr all dirty and messed up."

Navi stared at the man plain-faced. She didn't *want* to be walking through here all dirty and bare-footed. She started to realize the absurdity of walking into those apartments, hoping to find a friendly junkie to share their dope with her or perhaps a kind stranger who would give her some money to score something with. Maybe one of the thoughtful dealers would take pity on her and donate some dope to her worthy cause. She knew all of these scenarios were nonsense and she really didn't seem to have many options.

"What's wrong baby gurrl, can't you speak?" the sharp-dressed man asked her. "You sick or sumfin?" Navi stared back at him, doe-eyed, and slowly nodded her head up and down. "You dope-sick gurrl? You need yer fix now or what?" he asked. She just nodded her head in slow motion again. "Get in mah cadillac car and I'll get you cleaned up baby and I'll get you some good dope. Get on in hurr girl and let Daddy take care of you baby, we don't want you out hurr sick and dirty and bare footed."

Navi reached down and put her hand on the cold chrome door handle. She knew this was probably not the best thing she could do but she suddenly felt it was her only choice. This man obviously had some money, he was in a fancy car, dressed in fine clothes and had been smoking some pretty potent pot in his Swisher Sweet blunt. She knew he could afford to get her the dope she needed, and probably another room so she could clean herself up. Who knew, he may even buy her a new outfit and a pair of shoes.

He was staring her right in the eyes, that hand dangling over the steering wheel, just waiting for her to pull the door open and get in the car. He looked almost kind to her, like he really did want to help her. Like he really did care.

Navi took a deep breath and pulled the handle on the dark red door. As she sunk into the warm leather seat he hit the lever to put the dark tinted window up.

She exhaled slowly and turned to look at his face, keeping her eyes big and wide and trying to look as innocent as possible, hoping he would feel sorry for her and help her. "Baby, you done a good thing, it's a smart move getting in this cadillac car with Big Daddy. I'ma take care of you gurrl, don't you worry your pretty lil' head." Navi felt her heart stop as the door locks engaged when he pulled down on the gear shift. They slowly ambled out of the parking lot, onto the wide street and passed by the busy concrete apartment buildings.

As they drove off, Navi started to feel the familiar tinge of sickness in her stomach and the cramping in her arm, leg and back muscles. She put her hand over her belly and stared out the window, hoping with all the hope that she had left that this man was taking her to get her medicine.

Three

~

"INTO THE DARKNESS"

Navi was holding her belly, hoping her driver wouldn't hear the deep gurgling of her aching stomach. She felt the all-too-familiar sharp, shooting pains along her spine and a stabbing sensation in her gut. She really just wanted to get high and it seemed as if she was about to do whatever it took to do that.

"Baby Gurrl, you like smokin' that brown dope or that white dope?" asked the big, deep voice of her new companion. Navi turned her head to look at him with her big, wide eyes but she didn't answer. He pulled off the road and put the car in park. "Baby, you need to know I'm gunna take care of you, I'm your Daddy, Gurrl, and you're mah Baby Gurrl and I'ma take you to get your fix so you ain't sick no more, ya hear me? Daddy's gunna take real good care of you Baby Gurrl."

She just looked at him, motionless and silent. In her head she was running through all of the possible scenarios of what could happen to her as a result of getting herself into this crazy predicament. This man could rape her, hurt her, beat her, he could kill her. She could see any of those possibilities. Or, maybe he really did want to help her. Maybe he really just wanted to get her straight and didn't expect anything in return. Navi decided to believe that he was not the possible monster she had imagined but that he truly was just a nice man who was trying to help.

"It doesn't matter," she whispered.

"What did you say Baby Gurrl, you'll hafta speak up where yer Daddy can hear ya"

Navi cleared her dry, scratchy throat a little, "It really doesn't matter" she repeated.

"Hmmm, well a'ight'" he said as he dropped the gear shift back into drive and slowly pulled back out into traffic. He drove in silence to a little corner store with bars on the windows and ragged, sun bleached signs out front that were advertising off-brand cigarettes and malt liquor. "You stay right hurr girl, and don't you talk to anybody, don't even look at any of these fools, you hear me? I'ma go on in hurr and get you what you need gurrl. Daddy gunna take good care of his Baby Gurrl." Navi nodded, keeping her face down, staring at her tattered backpack resting on the floorboard by her feet.

He shut off the ignition, got out of the car and locked the doors. As Navi sat in the empty car she again began to imagine the terrible situations that could arise from this and started to feel a panic gripping her chest. With the windows all sealed and the doors locked, she started to feel like the air in this car was running out and a fat, hot tear rolled down one cheek and dripped onto the thin material draped over her chest. She could hear the voices and footsteps of the other young black men going in and out of the little shop but she didn't dare turn her gaze from that little ripped knapsack.

She sat alone in the leather seat and saw a picture flash through her mind of the darkness hovering over her earlier and the door to the little hotel room being kicked in. She recalled the fire flashing in the eyes of the gigantic man standing at the door and although now she knew he was a cop - someone who could punish her and lock her up - something in those eyes was almost kind. As scary as the whole situation had been, looking back now she could almost see how him showing up had actually been not such a bad thing after all.

Before she could think anymore about it, her driver returned. He was cradling a plain brown paper grocery bag with the top neatly folded down and when he got in the car he put it on the floorboard next to the backpack. Putting the key in the ignition, he looked forward and didn't say a word. After shifting the car into drive, he drove just a few blocks and turned in at the lovely Paradice Motel. He parked the car and again left all the windows up and doors locked. Navi stayed in the front seat of his cadillac, her eyes glued to the bags on the floor. He returned quickly and drove around to the back side of the long row of little clap-board buildings. Pulling up in front of the last room at the end of the building he parked the car in the little gravel lot and reached down, grabbing the paper sack.

"C'mon Baby Gurrl, you ready to get your medicine?" he asked her as he got out of the driver's seat.

Navi nodded her head and opened the door, finally stepping out of the car and putting her dirty feet on the sharp little rocks that made up her path to the doorway. She winced just a bit as the surprising pains shot up her legs but she managed to limp the short distance to the open door.

She had her head down and kept her eyes looking at the rocks beneath her feet, trying to be strategic in her steps to avoid the more jagged of the offenders. She felt just enough of the warmth of the sun on her back and shoulders to keep her from being too chilled by the early autumn breeze that was blowing her hair to one side. The sun was about to set and in the short time it took her to walk from the car to the doorway where her new companion was standing, that glowing ball started to hide itself behind the Paradice Motel sign on the other side of the building.

Navi crossed the threshold and went inside the room where he was waiting. As soon as she entered, he slammed the door shut behind her and the room filled with darkness. The thick drapes were tightly drawn around the room's one little window and not a bit of light entered the room through them. Navi's eyes worked to adjust to the sudden change and her heart was in her throat as a terrifying panic set in and she realized that she was indeed trapped.

She felt the roughness of her captor's calloused hand sliding up her arm and to her neck. Chills were racing up and down her spine and she stood frozen. He put his hand up to her face and touched her cheeks, brushing the back of his hand softly over each side but then quickly turning his hand over, he grabbed her jaws and pulled her to himself, putting his mouth completely over hers in a disgusting, coarse attempt at a kiss. Navi couldn't pull away, she couldn't move, she couldn't scream. She stood solid and still, static against his touch as he licked her mouth and face.

The man grabbed her around the waist and violently threw her in the general direction of the bed. Her head hit squarely on the corner of the nightstand and she instantly felt burning pain as a trickle of blood ran down her scalp and through her hair. The attacker gruffly dragged her rigid body across the bed, tugged off her jeans, and climbed on top of her. Navi felt a dread unlike any she had ever experienced and she held her breath tightly in her lungs, afraid to move a muscle.

She felt a sudden hot, blunt blow to her face as the man struck her with the back of his hand. He had used such force that it nearly knocked her out. Navi quickly gasped a lung-full of air and as the oxygen started racing through her body she felt the tingling sensations of pain all over her face, arms and legs. Again he struck her, this time with an open hand and with enough force to knock her completely out.

Navi felt like a rocket was propelling her backwards, away from her own body, as she quickly faded deep into the darkness.

Is this the truth You promised to me?
That sacred place
You hoped I'd reach?
Why can't I just let You be
and totally
take hold of me?

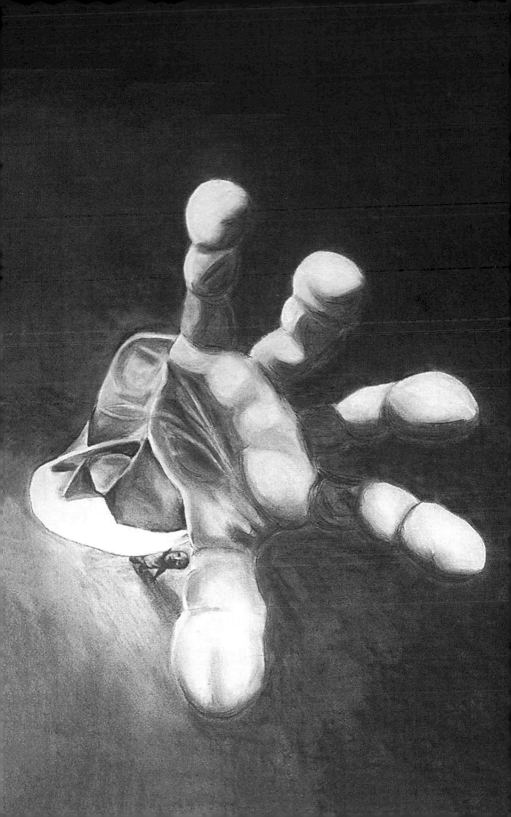

Four

~

"Binding Love"

While she was knocked out Navi had what could only be described as an out of body experience. When she was struck the second time, the impact sent her hurtling backwards through time and space. It was as if she were unfolding the layers of infinity, peeling one section back from another as her body raced at warp speed through the air. She could feel herself cutting away at the elastic-like separation that would normally prevent her from reaching through to eternity. It seemed as if infinite, incalculable hours passed in mere seconds. Her long hair was swirling behind her as her body was tunneling through the open expanse with such velocity that flames of white fire were flickering from her fingertips and toes.

Navi didn't know what this realm was that she had entered, but she suddenly felt fully alive. She knew that she had passed from the life she had been experiencing on the earth and entered into a new domain where no evil or defiled thing she had ever known could touch her. She was completely enveloped by a bright shining light which shone not only on her but also inside of her and was shining from within her all at once. She felt such tremendous peace and joy and love; each in the fullness of all that they are yet, more and more of themselves. Increasing, growing, expanding, the tangible love, joy and peace kept filling her up and pouring onto her in greater measure.

Feeling the intense warmth of the light and love and being overcome with pure joy, Navi began to laugh and sing as she twirled and spun through the atmosphere. Her heart was swelling and she felt so complete, so whole, as if she lacked nothing. As she twirled and laughed she felt the overwhelming presence of her Advocate, Defender and Friend as He came alongside her.

He wrapped Himself around her and hid her deep within His chest. She experienced an instant, exponential increase in her awareness of Love and Joy and allowed herself to be completely enveloped by the richness of His lovingkindness. As she found herself being buried in the abundance of Him and all He stands for, she became more and more aware that she indeed belonged to Him. Her desire to be removed from anything that would come between them grew as she wholly gave herself over to Him and all the fullness of who He is.

As He wrapped Himself around her even more, she felt the deepness of His protection and the safety of the hiding place within His bosom. He had completely covered her with His enormous arms and surrounded her whole body with the massive wings which protruded from His back. Even in the shadow of His wings the intensity of His light shone more and more and she felt His breath fill her lungs as the sharpness of His Love penetrated her heart. There was no pain felt but Navi still let out a loud wail that sounded like breaking glass and rushing water. Again He penetrated her heart, this time depositing His seed of Love deep inside her.

Navi was keenly aware that this moment was far-reaching. She realized that there was no time or space in the place where she stood with her Rescuer, but she knew everything that was happening was having an eternal effect on the earth.

He opened His wings and arms and pulled her up to His face. As He looked deeply into her eyes she understood that He fully knew her.

"I will never leave you," He said to her. "I will never be apart from you. I will be with you forever. My love for you binds Me to you."

Navi understood everything He said to her not in her mind, but in her heart that was now impregnated with the seed of His Love. Each individual word He uttered held it's full meaning and the truth of what He spoke cut her to the core. His words were alive and she didn't just hear them, but she could see them as shooting rays of light and feel them as warm ripples of joy that tickled against her skin. She could even smell the words as their honey-sweet fragrance wafted up to her nose. She discerned each of the words He had spoken and hid them away inside of her beating, gravid heart.

As swiftly as she had eclipsed time and space to arrive in this place with the Lover of her soul, she quickly plummeted back to the earth with such violent force that she could actually hear the atmosphere squealing as she transposed from one domain to another. Navi felt herself fall back into the shell of her body like a heavy weight being dropped from a tall building. She sat straight up and took a big, deep breath and opened her eyes wide. She was surrounded by utter darkness, a stark contrast to the radiant Light that had enveloped her only mere moments before. As she held her eyes open and moved her head from left to right she saw the faintest sliver of light peeking out from beneath a door in the far corner of the room.

Sitting still and silent, she listened intently in the inky black darkness and could hear muffled sounds of water running into a sink basin. Not taking her eyes from the thin slice of white light, she started to remember where she was and who she was with. Just as she started to get her bearings the door she had been staring at opened and what began as a slit became a deluge of light, flooding the room and causing Navi's eyes to twitch and throb.

Her captor stood in the doorway with his head down, looking almost like a little boy, ashamed and disheveled. He wouldn't raise his head to look at her but mumbled something incoherent and nodded toward the nightstand beside the bed. Navi slowly turned her head and saw the paper bag that he had carried in from the car but now it was all crumpled and wrinkled, not crisp and neat like it had been when he originally placed it between her feet on the floorboard of the cadillac.

Navi looked back at the big man who was casting a big shadow in the room. He picked his head up and sheepishly looked at her, almost flirtatiously. "Baby gurrl, you get cleaned up now. We gun hafta put your lil ass to work gurrl" he said to her.

She slowly sat up, feeling every joint and muscle in her body pop and creak, and she slid off the side of the bed, standing weakly before the crumpled brown bag. Reaching out towards it, she felt the sensations of burning and tingling in her right arm and shoulder but she extended it anyway, using her trembling hand to take hold of it, then turned and slowly crept toward the door and the light.

The man didn't move from her path, instead he stayed in the doorway watching her every move. Once Navi was before him he reached out and grabbed her face with his rough hand again. He licked all around her mouth and face and stuck his tongue in and out of her mouth, and at this point Navi felt so helpless and worthless she didn't even resist him. She heard a faint voice in her head telling her to run, but it was so much easier to just stand there and let him have his way.

"Baby gurl, you gun be mine forevah, you hurr me gurrl? Daddy ain't nevah gun let yer sweet lil ass get away. You gun stay with Big Daddy and I'm gunna take care a you gurrl, I'm gun watch you out on them streets and you gunna be mah gurrl. We gun go all over, gurrl, we be in Detroit and in Vegas, I'm gunna turn yer lil sweet ass out on all them streets gurrl. And you better never even think of runnin from yer Daddy, you better just keep wit me gurrl, cuz it's bad out thur and you need your Daddy takin care of you gurrl."

Navi pulled back from him but her chin was still in his grip. She stared back at him with those big doe-eyes and didn't say a word or move a muscle. The gruff brute held her face tightly in the grip of his coarse hand and tried to stare her down but quickly looked away. "Get yer ass ready, " he growled at her as he nudged her through the open door.

He walked away and sat on the bed, grabbed the remote and started flipping through the channels on the beat up old television and Navi slowly shut the door to the bathroom. She wanted to sit down on the toilet and cry her eyes out but she knew that would do no good. Even though she was scared to see her reflection, she took a deep breath and listlessly lifted her hand to the rusty metal frame of the medicine chest and slowly pushed it closed, taking care not to make too much sound.

Navi gasped when she saw the reflection of her right arm in the warped mirror. No wonder it had been stinging and tingling, her tricep was one big purple bruise! She tried to turn her back toward the reflection enough to see the whole black and blue mark, but it spread all the way across her shoulder and onto her back, so it was impossible for her to see its entire range. Her already ragged tank top was literally hanging on her by threads and had been torn into long strips that barely covered her body.

She suddenly felt like a piece of meat, just a pile of flesh that had been thrashed around and pushed against and penetrated and thrown about. She wanted to scream and she wanted so badly to run, but she remembered the strength of her captor and how with just one sharp back-handed smack he had sent her into another dimension.

Oh! That alternate dimension! That other world she had experienced! Was that a reality or a result of her delusional unconsciousness? She suddenly felt a warm, rich wave of love and light wash over her and had a momentous feeling of peace that centered her and gave her the sense she needed to stay aware of where she was.

Navi set the brown bag on the lid of the toilet and pulled apart the top of the crumpled paper to reveal the contents. Reaching into the sack, she pulled out a stained denim mini skirt, a small, thin white button-up men's oxford shirt, a pair of little white ankle socks with lace around the tops, and a pair of size 8 black patent leather pumps. Stuck in the folds of brown paper in the bottom of the bag were two little blue hair barrettes, a used stub of a black eyeliner and a red lipstick sample like they give away at the department stores when a lady gets a makeover.

Having no doubt or misunderstanding of what was expected of her, Navi started running hot water in the sink so she could clean up and change her clothes. She had been given little outfits to put on before, but it had been quite some time ago when she was just learning about how to use her body to get people to do things for her. Back then it was always something brand-new, nice and pretty; a lacy new nightie or silky slip that she would find laid out on her pink princess canopy bed. She would quickly change into her new outfit, then come and model for her daddy and his friends. They would give her fruity rum drinks, then do a photoshoot or make a movie of her acting like a pretty little lady in her pretty new nightgown. After she would get her pictures taken in the nightie, they would take pictures of each other touching her and doing things to her. But those things usually didn't bother her too much after she drank the fruity drinks. And, Navi had practiced all of this by acting out the things she had been shown in movies of other little girls with their daddies and his friends.

As the water got hotter Navi took a ragged washrag from the metal rack by the shower and dipped it into the sink. She quickly unwrapped the paper from a thin sliver of soap laying beside the sink and let it fall into the basin and started swirling the water. Shutting off the faucet and feeling the hot, burning sensation of the scalding water, she watched as both her hands turned dark red. Plucking the cloth out of the steaming washbowl, she rang out all the water and rubbed the searing rag over her pale face. Dropping the towel back into the water, she quickly slid out of her tattered clothes and used the hot wash rag to scrub herself in the places she felt most dirty, like between her legs and under her arms. The whole time she took great care not to strain her bruised right arm and shoulder too much.

Once she had her body cleaned up, Navi started putting on the outfit she had pulled out of the bag. Sliding the little blue skirt over her slender hips and pulling the oxford over her arms and around her chest, she zipped up the skirt and buttoned the top few buttons on the shirt, then tightly tied it's tails at her waist, leaving the knot above her navel so her slim belly showed. She bent over the toilet and tugged the socks onto her dirty, stained feet and slid them into the half-a-size-too-big pumps.

After she had the outfit on, Navi set to pulling her hair back with the little blue clips and did her best to use the make up to rouge her cheeks and darken her lips and eyes. As she finished up with her face and hair she felt that unmistakable tinge in her stomach telling her that it was, indeed, time for her medicine. She took one last look at herself in the mirror and gave herself a little mental pep-talk, telling herself if she was just an obedient, good girl and didn't fight this man and try to get away that he would live up to his promise to her and give her the dope she was so sick for. Taking a long, deep breath she turned to the door and pulled it open, standing upon the same threshold the crude man had graced just ten short minutes before.

"Damn baby gurrl, you sure do clean up right! Shoot gurrl, look at choo, you looking good gurrl! Come over hurr an let Daddy see how sweet you look gurrl," he bayed at her.

Navi kept her eyes on the ground as she walked toward the bed he had sprawled himself out on. She was still unable to look at him in the face but she came right up next to him and let him grab her around the waist and pull her to himself.

"Gurrl, you lookin and smellin so sweet. Let me tell you right now, yer ass belongs to me, I'm yer Big Daddy, you hurr me gurrl? You betta look at me gurrl!"

Navi was scared and quickly turned her head to look him square in the face in terror.

"You betta look at me gurrl but I'm tellin ya right now, if anotha playa comes around and you look him in the eye I'll snap yer neck and I ain't lyin. You betta do just what I tell yer ass to do and keep yer eyes on me, you hurr me gurrl?"

Navi nodded her head up and down slowly, her big eyes fixed on his.

Sliding his hand shrewdly up the back of her little skirt, he grabbed the top of her thigh and shook her whole body. "You hurr me gurrl? You ever gunna look at anotha one of those playas? Answer yer pimp, trick!" he shouted at her.

"No" Navi mumbled as he glared at her trembling face.

"Say. 'No Daddy, I promise.'" he demanded.

"No Daddy I promise" Navi repeated.

"That's a good gurrl. You gunna do good out hurr on this track, you gunna bring yer Daddy some big money, trick." He growled at her, taking his hand from her backside and reaching onto the nightstand to grab a little, brown paper bag, the size a child would pack a lunch in to take to school.

He opened the top of the bag and let Navi see inside. All she needed was in that brown sack! It was like a junkie's first-aid kit with a brand new pipe, filter, lighter and most importantly, a tiny baggie full of little brownish-white rocks. She could feel the warm sensations of cravings trailing up and down her body and all at once her stomach turned over on itself. Lunging forward toward the little plastic trashcan next to the nightstand, she threw up what stomach acids were left in her empty belly.

Standing up and wiping her mouth with the back of her hand she suddenly had no problem looking her captor right in the eye and turning on the charm. He had what she wanted, and she was willing to give him whatever he wanted to get a hold of it. Putting on her shiest, most sheepish smile and batting her big eyes, she cooed at him, "Is that for me?"

"Trick, you know that's yer dope, I ain't messin around smokin no junk. But you ain't gettin dis dope till you git out on that track an earn it. I ain't sendin mah brand new baby gurrl out on dem streets all smoked out an high."

Navi realized at that moment that this was a game, but they weren't exactly pitted against one another. Rather, they were on the same team, working together to satisfy their individual longings. Right now this man was in control, but if she gave him what he was demanding, she would get what she wanted. Which was exactly what she intended to do. And because she got to make the first move, she was technically in control, since she would determine how long the process of obtaining the object of her desire would take. She was so dope sick that she was willing to do anything he required in order to get those drugs into her system.

"You ready to turn dem tricks, gurrl?"

Taking a deep breath, Navi slowly nodded her head up and down. "Yes, daddy." she said, keeping her eyes big and round, fixed on his.

The man put the paper bag in the drawer of the night stand and as he stood up, he put his big hand on her bruised shoulder and squeezed. He spun her around and, opening the door, steered her over the threshold into the pitch black night.

Five

~

"Tricky, Tricky"

A s they walked through the gravel parking lot in silence, Navi started to feel a connection and a strange comradery with this man. She was beginning to understand how this life would work; she would go make money and bring it back to him in exchange for dope. It really seemed easy and started to make perfect sense in her mind.

As they neared the end of the row of buildings they had been walking along, the man spoke to her in a low, hushed voice. "Gurl, you go git yer big daddy some cheese, you betta go make me $500 tonight. You hit that quota and we'll go back to our room so you can get smoked out, ya hurr me?"

Turning the corner, they were on the main drag that ran in front of Paradice Motel now. The street lights lining the track were sporadic and it seemed that only every other one or so was even functioning. Many of the ratty motels along this strip had rickety neon signs that either flashed intentionally or flickered on and off as if the bulbs were about to wear out. Navi was surprised at how many women she saw, at least one or two on each corner and even more walking up the sidewalks or leaning against buildings. As cars slowly drove up or down the four lane road, some of the women would intentionally cross the street in front of the head lights, strutting themselves with their shoulders pushed back and their hind ends stuck out.

"Trick, you stay right hurr on this corner and if you git a john who wants a room, you tell him yer daddy said he's gotta git a room hurr at the Paradice, ya hurr me? You betta not be goin off wit no man for less than fifty dollars, ya hurr me? You brand new out on this track and you lookin good, gurrl."

Navi didn't really understand what he meant by any of the things he said, but she nodded and kept scanning the street, taking in the scene that was unlike anything she had ever seen before.

"Daddy gunna be right back hurr watchin out fer his baby gurrl, ya hurr me? Ain't no one gunna hurt you gurrl, I gotcha and ain't no one gunna take you nowhere, ya hurr me? Go git mah money an we'll go back in our room so you can smoke."

With that, he stepped back into the shadows and left Navi all alone on the street corner.

She didn't really know what to do and just stood there, still holding her arms down stiffly at her sides and peering down the long, wide street. Navi was scared to death but she didn't show it. Instead, she took a deep breath and a big step back so she could lean her back against the building. She closed her eyes and wanted to throw her head back and scream but instead she swallowed hard and forced the huge lump down that had formed in her throat.

Standing there in the chill of night, she felt so alone, so vulnerable, so helpless. Big tears started to well up in her eyes and she could tell she was on the verge of completely losing it. She felt she was at the absolute lowest place in her life, totally worthless, just like a piece of trash.

At that very moment a carload of loud teenage boys sped by and blared their horn, shouting insults at Navi and throwing a bag of fast food wrappers and trash at her. They laughed as they tossed a big paper cup filled with soda at the ground in front of her. She tried to jump to the side to avoid being sprayed with the sticky liquid, but she still got soaked all down her right side. She felt the icy cold, syrupy soda pop running down her legs and causing one side of the white oxford to cling to her like a drippy second skin.

The hooting and hollering faded away as they drove off and Navi just stood there in total shock. Her hair had gotten sprayed and was pasted to the side of her face and as the lines of half-frozen liquid traced down her cheek, the gate holding back the rush of those big, hot tears broke wide open and she started bawling and crying, right there under the golden glare of the fading street light.

Just as quickly as that car full of delinquents had sped by her, Navi felt big, rough hands grab her shoulders and before she knew it she was snatched up and drug back into the dark alley. The calloused hands spun her around and as her eyes began to adjust to the darkness, she could start to make out the face of her pimp. As soon as it registered in her mind that he had ahold of her, she felt the intense blow of the back of his left hand smacking the side of her face.

That was all it took for her to be sent back through that tunnel of light once again, but now she happily fell back into the warmth and light that she had gotten familiar with the last time he had knocked her out. This time it was a much quicker journey, and before she even realized what was happening, she was in the presence once again of that Person of Love.

He was radiantly glowing and shining so brightly! She would have gone blind if she had beheld him with the human eyes she would have used to gaze at him if he had been standing upon the earth. But they were in the cosmic, seemingly magical place once again and it was all she could do just to look at him. Navi knew that this Man was her King, her Champion and she felt so alive and at ease in His presence.

As he stood before her, she could feel the light that was radiating off of him beginning to penetrate her. This man was not like any man she had ever known. She could tell that he was at once kind yet strong, he was gentle yet somehow she knew that he could destroy her, he could destroy everything she had ever known. But even as intense and powerful as he was, Navi was not at all afraid of him. She instead stood mesmerized in his presence.

The glow that was on him seemed to pulsate and carry the rhythm of his heartbeat. In some strange way Navi could just tell that his heart was beating for her. She just knew that the man had such a deep love and affection towards her and the longer she was near him, the more she realized that he was getting inside of her.

She was fully at ease, accepting all of this love and light that he was transferring into her. As she received the good things he was putting inside of her, she was being transformed on the inside. Navi the girl may be laying in a muddy puddle with her skirt hiked up, face down in a dark alley off of a sketchy inner-city street corner, but Navi the spirit was being healed and loved and expanded. He was growing his love inside of her, incubating a seed of love that had been hidden in her heart years before.

The love kept coming in waves and each time the sensation passed over her, Navi leaned farther forward. She couldn't get enough of the love and she wanted to embrace it, to become one with it. More and more love was washing over her and she was pressing into it harder with all the force she had. The man reached out to her with both hands and she fell into his loving arms, finally crashing her whole body into him.

He wrapped her in his big, strong arms and though he was holding her tightly, he remained gentle and easy, as if she were a delicate piece of porcelain. As he held her she could feel the love tunneling directly from his heart into hers at such a rapid pace that everything around them started to spin outward at breakneck speeds.

"Navi, I love you. You are precious to me," he said to her. "I will be with you everywhere you go. I will never be apart from you, I will always love you."

As he spoke those words, Navi broke free from his grasp. Feeling that love was one thing but hearing it was another. She was processing the words he said through her wounded mind that had been so filled with rejection and pain her entire life. All of these things he said about always being there and loving no matter what were quite foreign to her.

By breaking free of the hold he had on her, Navi backed into the spinning vortex that had surrounded them and she started spinning out away from him. At once she felt herself fading out of that realm and suddenly - wham! - she fell back into her body, face-down in the mud.

She could tell that the rough, gruff man was standing over her and she could hear him hurling insults at her and saying crazy things about her being his property, about owning her and never letting her go.

"Gurrl, I told you! You're mine forever! I ain't never gunna let yer nasty, dirty lil ass go! Yer gonna stay wit

Daddy and bring me mah money, gurrl! Get yer ugly butt up off tha ground, gurrl, or I'm gunna knock you out again! And you better git up and git out on that track and get mah money, trick!"

Navi rolled over on her side and opened her eyes. It was dark in the alley but the light coming off the street was just enough to help her see where she laid. She saw the corner of a dumpster directly in her line of vision, about 6 or 8 feet in front of her. As she looked down from that point toward where the alley met the street she could see the orange haze of the old streetlights glowing and watched as the silhouettes of a pair of tall, skinny girls crossed in front of the alley wearing mini skirts and stiletto heels.

Her line of vision darkened as the shadow of the pimp came over her. He stood himself between her and the rectangle of orange light and nearly blocked out the glow completely. Navi didn't move or lift her eyes, she just laid completely still on the cold, muddy ground, holding her breath and not even daring to blink. She could make out the distinct outline of his right foot in a size 12 Timberland steel-toed boot. As soon as her brain registered that he had pulled his foot back, she felt herself flying backwards and slamming her head into the corner of the dumpster.

"Ho! I told you git yer ass up an git out on dat track! I ain't wastin anymore time wit you! You go git me mah money ho!"

Navi curled herself up into a ball and started crying. She had never been so afraid and her head banging the corner of the dumpster had caused a sharp, ringing pain that just amplified her fear.

Her tormenter took two long strides to once again stand over her. She had turned as she flew backwards and now the light was completely behind her and if there had been even a sliver peeking through, he would be over-shadowing it now.

"Git UP, ho!" he growled at her through his clenched teeth in a most threatening way.

Navi stopped her sobs and stiffened her body up. She knew what he was capable of now and didn't want to endure another boot to the stomach. She slowly turned herself to lay on her front so she could start to pick herself up from the muddy ground. She placed the palms of her hands on the ground, directly below her shoulders and pushed herself up. The higher she raised her head the louder her ears rang but she kept pushing, digging the palms of her hands and her bony knees into the damp asphalt. As the ringing increased, her world started spinning and she lost her balance, falling from the half-way up position she had reached to being once again on the ground, catching herself on her elbows and then falling off to the side.

The pimp stooped down over her and grabbed the back of her now muddy and stained oxford shirt and yanked her up to her feet. She was woozy with the pain and the suddenness of standing and she actually leaned into him for support and to stable herself. As she buried her head in his chest he stepped back from her.

"Ho, don't be rubbin all yer snotty muddy face on me, I aint yer hankie! Straighten yo self up gurrl, you got some work to do! Git out thur on dat track and make me some money!"

Navi balanced herself on her scuffed up little patent leather shoes, smoothed out her hair and then rubbed her hands down the front of her little plaid skirt. Running the back of her hand over her cheek, she could feel the mud being smeared across her face. Her face, stomach and arm were aching and throbbing and there was a sharp pain shooting across the back of her head.

Now that she had fully experienced the level of anger this man could display, she was fully aware that her best choice to stay alive and in one piece would be to just do whatever he told her to do. So she lowered her eyes and with her head down she turned from him and started shuffling her feet, allowing them to carry her towards the rectangle of orange light spilling into the alley. She could hear him mumbling behind her, his angry voice becoming more muffled and distant the further she shuffled away from him.

Once Navi made it back out to the street corner, she realized that if she ever wanted to get high again she was just going to have to do what he wanted her to do. And, after what she had just been through, getting high was her one and only thought. She took one more deep breath, cocked her shoulders back, stuck her rear end out and sauntered out into the street to put herself on display for all to see.

Six

~

"Mourning Moon"

I t certainly didn't take long for Navi to make an impression out on the grisly street. As she sashayed across the pavement a gold sedan slowed way down and crawled past her, the window open and the outline of a man's face hiding in the dark cabin. Navi had barely made it to the sidewalk on the opposite side of the street and he swung around in a wide U-turn to pull up along the curb, right next to her. As he lowered the window, she bent down and stuck her head in, resting her arms along the door frame over her head.

The man was small and very well dressed, an Asian with thick black hair and a fine, expensive watch. He was probably in his early 50's and seemed kind and shy. Navi just looked at him with the best innocent, doe-eyed face she could muster, waiting for the man to have the first word.

"Um, hello" he said quietly, seeming to stammer over even those two simple words. He sheepishly looked away.

"Are you available?" he asked. His accent was strong and he kept his head down and his eyes looking at the tops of his hands folded neatly in his lap.

"Mm-hmm" Navi purred, keeping her eyes fixed on him.

"Where we should go?" the man asked, turning to look at her again. Navi pointed back to the other side of the street where the Paradice Motel sign was flickering.

"OK, I meet you there" he said, reaching up to put the car in drive.

Navi pulled herself up and away from the side of the car and started walking back over to the dark alley that led to the dingy motel. As she stepped into the darkness she felt such a lurching in her stomach that she instantly doubled over and vomited along the side of the building. All that came up was stomach acids and saliva, and it burned her throat as it gushed out. She heaved three or four more times, crouching down with one hand holding her hair back from her face and the other against the cold cinder block wall in front of her.

"Trick, you best git yerself together and go git dat man's money. Don't you let 'em touch you for less than fiddy, ho. Ya hear me?" She could hear the pimp grumbling at her from the other side of the alley. He was standing next to the dumpster she had recently collided with.

Straightening up, Navi wiped the back of her hand over her mouth and started walking toward the parking lot at the other end of the alley. She felt as if she was walking to her death, the steps growing longer and more hollow the closer she came to the gravel parking lot. If this was her own funeral that she was walking into, the end of her life was pretty sad. This was the absolute lowest of the lowest of the lows and she was crossing into something she had always swore she would never do.

As she stepped into the lit-up, open space at the edge of the alley she saw the gold sedan parked 20 yards from her. Walking up onto the sidewalk that ran in front of the motel rooms, she saw the short, Asian man standing in a doorway, timidly looking down at his shoes.

Navi picked up her pace and trotted over to where he stood with the door opened. She ducked past him and entered the room and was surprised at what she saw inside.

"This must be the 'honeymoon suite'" she thought as she surveyed the room. The walls and carpet were both a drastic carnation pink, and standing in the room felt like looking out from inside of a bottle of Pepto Bismol. The heavy drapes covering the small window beside the door she had came through were made of a faded pink and purple patterned fabric dating back to long before she was born and the ratty blanket thrown on the lumpy bed looked like it was from the same edition but had been laundered so many times the colors had been all but washed away.

Navi really had no idea what to expect from the man nervously standing by the door, but she knew he could never hurt her anymore than she had already suffered. She asked him plainly what he wanted her to do and simply complied. He knew exactly what he wanted and that made it easy for her. The lights stayed on and everything was over really quickly, much to the relief of the both of them.

Once everything was finished the man handed her three $100 dollar bills. Navi could barely grasp what had just happened but she almost felt proud once she held the money in her hands. In his broken English, the man asked if he could take pictures of her shoes and Navi obliged him, although she couldn't see why he would want a photo of her ragged, mud stained socks and scuffed up shoes, but he took two pictures and then gave her two more $100 bills.

They left the room hurriedly, the man got into his sedan and drove off with his head down as Navi walked back to the alley where she knew the big pimp was waiting for her. She never even considered trying to hide any of the money or keeping it for herself, she just walked right up to him and handed all five bills over to him.

"Damn gurrl! That China-man gave you all this?!" he exclaimed. Navi just nodded silently, not sure what she would say to him if she was to open her mouth.

"Then you best git out on that track and see ten more dates tonite! I wanna see you git all dat money, ho! You go git yerself out on dat corner! You gunna clean up out on this track tonight!" he said as he pushed her toward the street again.

Navi did what he told her to and walked down the alley to stand under the flickering street light. None of what the other streetwalkers said or did had any effect on her and she didn't even notice the cars passing by. She felt like she was in a bubble or a dream, as if everything was happening all around her. If she was laid out on a gurney the paramedics standing over her would declare her "non-responsive."

In the midst of her stupor, seeing past the hazy glow of neon she caught a glimpse of the moon shining brightly in the highest part of the night sky. She gazed at the pulsating orb and saw it in this moment differently than she had ever seen it before - it almost seemed to be alive, like the giant glowing soul of a man perched high above her and the sadness and sorrow of this lonely street. The moon didn't seem sad like the street, but it did seem to be groaning, as if it were anticipating something. She thought for an instant that maybe the moon was mourning.

Something grabbed her attention back at the street level and her eyes shifted from the sky above to the road before her. A car had pulled up in front of her and lowered the passenger window. Not sure if she was still in a sort of dream state, she hesitantly walked to the curb and bent down to peer inside.

One look at the driver was all it took to send her back into full alert. Navi recognized instantly that this was the policeman who had busted down the door when that icky black thing was smothering her. She couldn't even begin to comprehend what he would be doing here on this street corner, trying to pick her up like a john picking up a hooker. Neither of them said a word but Navi opened the door and in her astonishment she slid herself into the passenger seat, not taking her eyes off the man even for a moment.

"Don't worry, Navi," he said to her in a deep, rumbling voice. "I will give you money to take back to him so he won't beat you when I drop you off."

Navi did not know how to even comprehend what was happening. She KNEW this man was the police officer, but she wanted to ask him if he really was. She wanted to ask him what that black thing was that had been smothering her. She wanted to ask him how he knew where to find her; she wanted to ask him how he knew that man would beat her if she didn't bring him money; she wanted to ask him how he knew her name?

But, she sat silently in the passenger seat, her eyes absolutely glued on the huge, dark-skinned man. She didn't dare utter a single word. She didn't even make a sound.

"Navi, what were you looking at a moment ago?" he asked her as he pulled the gear shifter down and moved slowly away from the curb.

Navi was silent, still staring at him in shock.

"What were you looking at, child?" he asked again, but this time his deep, chocolate voice tinged with just enough sweetness to build the tiniest bit of trust in her.

"The moon." she answered in a hushed voice.

"What did you see in the moon? How would you describe it?" he asked, taking his eyes off the road just long enough to look her in the face as he awaited a response.

"It looked sad and alone. Like a widow at her husband's funeral," she replied.

"Ah, yes. That is the perfect way to describe it. You are right, Navi. The moon is mourning and waiting. Waiting for you, Navi. Waiting for you to be fully revealed."

These words didn't just rest on the girl, they sunk down deep into her being. She didn't really understand what he was saying, but his word over her that something was waiting for her, that anything or anyone was concerned for her or even interested in her - that impacted her in a deep way.

They went on for the next several minutes in silence. The man was driving her further and further from the neon lit street and before she knew it, they were In a dark, open place along the river. Along the other side of the mighty river were twinkling lights, and the moon was still shining over them, but the place they had entered was dark, quiet and still. The man put his vehicle in park and invited Navi to step out with him.

Acting as quite the gentleman, he quickly went around to her side so he could open her door and offer his hand as she exited the car. As she stood up next to him, Navi was struck with awe at how large he was. This man was literally almost 9 feet tall and his hand was as big as her entire torso. His eyes were flashing with lights and she felt as if she had seen him before, somewhere other than in that hotel room that day he chased the black darkness away. She felt as if she'd looked into those lightning-flashing eyes before. She felt as if he already knew her, as if he knew everything about her just by looking at her with his lightning-eyes.

Grabbing her around the waist, he swiftly spun her around to face the opposite direction. "Navi, this is the dividing line. This is the place where you make a choice."

She really had no idea what he was talking about but she knew what he was saying had been waiting to be said for years.

"Do you believe that you can cross through that river and come out clean on the other side?"

Navi looked at the wide, flowing river and then looked up into the man's flashing eyes. "I don't know," she said softly, her lack of confidence causing her shoulders to slump and her head to hang low.

"Navi, do you believe that I can carry you across that river?"

She looked up at him again, taking notice of just how BIG he really was. His arms were each bigger than her entire body. His legs met his hips at her shoulder-height. She figured if anyone could carry a girl across that river-bed it would be this giant of a man.

"Yes, I think you probably can," she answered sheepishly.

"Do you believe that I could stop the water from flow-ing and stack it up on either side like giant walls, allowing you to walk through the bottom of the riverbed on dry ground?"

As crazy as that sounded, Navi was more apt to believe he could do that than carry her. She wouldn't forget that she had witnessed him throw that blackness through the wall, and she felt like this man already knew her, like he was setting her up with each question he asked. Any min-ute she expected him to say, "This is what you thought about that day when you went to the park as a little six-year-old girl, or, 'Remember, this happened in that book you read in 4th grade."

Navi raised her head to look up at his glowing face once more and said confidently, "Yes. I believe you could do that," but looking away quickly she muttered, "but I don't know why you would."

In an instant the man was down at her eye-level. He took her face in his hands and gazed deep into her eyes. She could feel nothing but his love radiating into her as he spoke deep, loving words that penetrated her heart. "Navi, I can do that for you and I would. I love you with an everlasting love and nothing you ever do or say will change that. There will be a day soon when you fully receive my love and all of the benefits that come with it. On that day you will walk through the raging river on dry ground and come out clean on the other side."

Picking her up in his massive arms, he started spinning her around as tears flowed from both of their eyes. Navi's head was buried right under his chin & she was cocooned in his embrace. As the tears fell, the big hot drops ran over her head and saturated her hair, running down her shoulders and eventually soaking her whole body. He held her tightly along the banks of that river, sewing their souls together with this matchless love.

It seemed like Navi was wrapped in his arms for an eternity, and after some time passed, he started telling her again how much he loved her. The more he said it, the harder it was for her to hear. She climbed out of his embrace and stood on the ground, turning her back to him.

"Can we go back now?" Navi asked. "I know that man is waiting for me."

He knew exactly why she wanted to go back, and the last reason was to get back to the abusive pimp. He knew she wasn't able to hear the words of love and affirmation he had been speaking over her. And he knew she was thinking about that folded-over brown paper bag. She wanted the drugs to start flowing through her again so the self-rejection and hatred would get tuned out and numbed away.

"Navi, get in the car and I will take you back to that hotel, and to that man." he said firmly. "This can wait for your tomorrow."

Navi avoided eye contact with him as she climbed back into the car. They drove back into the city in silence as the big orange moon hovered over the buildings downtown, highlighting the huge pyramid-shaped building along the river.

The naive young girl didn't even know what it meant, but playing over and over like a broken record in her head, she heard the phrase "going back to Egypt."

Is this the light You shine on me?
In the darkness
I couldn't see.
Why can't I just let You be
and totally
be redeemed?

Seven

~

"TUNE IN & TURN OUT"

*T*hey arrived at the street corner where he had picked her up and the man told Navi to look in the trash can in front of the liquor store he was dropping her off at. He said she would find some money to give to the man who was waiting for her, but Navi was more than a little scared to get out of the car without getting the money. She knew after being gone so long the pimp was sure to smack her if she came back empty handed, but for some reason she really did believe there would be money in the trash can. When she got out of the car, she walked right up to the front of the liquor store, not looking back at all or even saying goodbye.

Almost instantly, and quite comically, she saw a stack of fifty dollar bills laying in a neat pile right on top of the garbage. She picked them up and scurried her way across the street and into the alley where she knew the pimp was waiting for her.

She didn't even bother to count the money or anything, she just walked right up to him and handed it all over.

The pimp started exclaiming about how much money was there and how he had never seen a white girl pop her cherry out here like this, bringing in over $5000 in one night. Navi didn't stick around to listen to him, she just kept walking down the hazy alley, making a beeline for the hotel room. The pimp realized she had kept going and he turned to follow her. Once they got to the little room, he pulled the key out and unlocked the door to the dark and dirty lair.

When Navi flipped on the light switch there was a black flash across the entire floor of the room as most of the cockroaches retreated to underneath the bed or cabinets. There were a few that were defiant, as if they weren't so scared of the humans entering the room that they would need to run and hide. They just seemed to stare up at Navi and her pimp, rubbing their little antennae together and crouching down close to the floor.

Navi had been through so much this evening that she wasn't even fazed by the nasty little intruders. She had one thing on her mind, and it was in that paper bag hiding in the drawer of the nightstand by the bed. As she went towards it to open the drawer, she was caught mid-step, stopped dead in her tracks. The big pimp had reached out and grabbed the back of the shirt she was wearing and pulled her back to himself.

"Ho, I know full well you ain't thinkin you'll just roll up in dis room and git all smoked out??! You ain't makin these rules, trick! You'll smoke when I tell you to smoke!"

He shoved her down on the bed and she landed on the shoulder that had been so badly bruised earlier. She didn't wince or even whimper, though. Instead, she just kept her eyes on the drawer of that nightstand and kept her thoughts fixed on packing that pipe and taking a big, long hit.

She knew he was standing over her yelling, but she couldn't hear what he was saying. She could tell he was smacking her and shaking her, but she had gone completely numb. She just laid on the bed with her eyes fixed on the drawer of the little night stand. Everything else was a blur.

Once he was done screaming at her and slapping her around a bit, the violent man reached to the nightstand and took out the little brown bag. Navi sat straight up in the bed and her eyes filled with tears. She wanted what was in that bag so badly. She knew it was the only thing in the world that could take away the shame and sadness she felt after what she had done that night.

"Here, trick. Hurry up and git yer fix." He grumbled as he tossed the bag next to her on the bed. He continued to grumble and growl about how he hated baseheads and it was so nasty to see a girl get all turned out on that junk as he made his way to the bathroom and shut the door, closing himself inside and leaving Navi alone with the prize she had lusted after all night.

The girl could hardly believe this was really happening. She was excited and nervous at the same time and felt almost as if she would throw up due to the anticipation of getting to smoke again. She quickly opened the bag and dumped all the contents out on the bed. As she worked to prep the pipe and pack it full with a big, sticky hit of dope she noticed the little junky television sitting on top of the old dresser in the corner had an FM radio dial running along the side of it. She always enjoyed getting high so much more when she had some soft music playing, so she walked over and fiddled with the dials until she found the R&B station and left it playing really low.

Making her way back to the bed, pipe in hand the whole time, she picked up the lighter and assumed the position to take what would be the first, magnificent hit she had taken in days, but right as she was about to put the pipe to her lips the radio started to blare static loudly through the speakers. Navi went back across the room and stood next to the tv and twisted the volume knob to turn down the loud static noise, but when she was standing there, the static stopped and the soft urban music started crooning out again. She stood there, leaning slightly against the dresser, lifted the pipe again and prepared to take that glorious hit, when all of a sudden that loud static came blaring out of the speakers.

With that, Navi quickly decided she wasn't nearly as interested in hearing music as she was in smoking that dope so she switched the radio dial to off. Now, in her perfectly quiet sanctuary she would finally be able to smoke in peace. She lifted the pipe once again and just as she put it to her lips, the bathroom door opened and that giant ogre of a man lazily migrated to the bed. With one swipe of his arm he swept the paper sack and baggie of dope Navi had left strewn across the comforter onto the floor. That had Navi frantic, and instead of taking that hit she darted back to the bedside to pick up her prized jewels.

As she picked the greasy rocks from the filthy carpet she heard the pimp telling her to hurry up and he thought she would be done by now. He told her she would sleep on the floor tonight like the nasty dog she was, down on the floor digging for crumbs. Navi collected all the little lint-covered treasures from the carpet and went back over to the dresser where she dumped them in a little pile, then once again lifted up that pipe.

Navi had the pipe in one hand and the lighter in the other and she was about to marry the two and finally feel that sweet and sour numbness she had so badly been craving for so long. Just as she was about to take that big, gratifying hit, the radio started loudly blaring static again. It startled Navi and jolted the man straight up from the bed. Unable to even think straight, she fumbled the dials again and made sure they were all still turned to the off position. She couldn't understand why the radio was roaring with all the switches and knobs in the off position, so she quickly reached behind the dresser and pulled the plug, but that didn't seem to work. The static just got louder and louder.

The man leapt over to her side and pulled the ratty cord from behind the dresser. He was shocked to see the plug was pulled but the sound was still loudly pouring out of the speakers. Not knowing what else to do, he thrust the tv off the dresser and busted it. Now the room was stone-cold quiet and he and Navi just stared at each other, eyes as big as saucers and hearts pounding wildly.

Navi still gripped that glass stem tightly in her hand. She was disturbed by what had just happened but was not prepared to put the pipe down. She had gone through too much to turn it away now. All of the sordid events of her recent past started flooding into her mind. Above the clamoring of all she had seen, heard and experienced these past few days the only rational thought she could muster was that it would all be a waste if she gave up now and didn't partake of the sweet elixir she had finally gotten her hands on.

With the pimp standing right beside her and their eyes fixed on each other, Navi again brought the pipe up to her pursed lips. She could anticipate the wave of ecstasy that was about to wash over her body and she flicked the lighter and brought the flame up to her face.

Just then, much like the first few times, the radio started blaring out again. But, this time it was different.

Unexplainably, from the shattered pile of busted plastic and tangled wire guts, the radio again blared out an ear shattering static sound and then a man's voice became audible, saying over and over, "Break the calf, break the calf, break the calf....."

Navi let loose a blood curdling scream, turned and ran out of the hotel room. She stood in the gravel parking lot and faced the open door, the glass pipe clenched so tightly in her hand it should have broken, but she held it high over her head and kept screaming. The pimp came and stood at the threshold of the room, his face full of fear. That eerie voice kept chanting from the broken radio, "Break the calf, break the calf, break the calf..." and Navi responded by thrusting the glass pipe down on the narrow concrete sidewalk, wailing as it shattered into a million pieces.

The pimp rushed to his cadillac, pulling Navi by the arm to drag her with him. He opened the passenger door and pushed her in, then ran around to the drivers' door and jumped behind the wheel. With one fluid motion he turned the ignition and threw the car into reverse, spewing gravel everywhere as he sped out of the parking lot and skidded sideways into the street. Navi was crying, tears soaking her face, sobs erupting from deep within her chest as she moaned and wailed, terrified by what she had just experienced.

The pimp was silent, still shaking off the fear that had rocked him to his very core. He didn't want to believe what he had just witnessed and as much as he wanted to deny what had happened, he knew it was real. For some reason, he kept thinking about when he was a little boy and what his Mammy used to tell him about a man named Moses breaking two stone tablets and a golden cow.

Eight

"This is Your Tomorrow"

*N*avi's head was spinning, but the more distance the driver put between the cadillac and the Paradice Motel, the easier it was for her to slow her sobs and wails. Eventually she quit crying all together and just stared out the passenger window, her face wet with the snot and tears.

Her driver had calmed his nerves as well, but he was still worked up and his mind was racing. He tried to get a grip on his thoughts, but he just gripped the steering wheel tighter as he tried to swallow the lump in his throat. Even more perplexing to him was the memory of his Mammy. In the same way a dope addict keeps their painful memories numbed out by getting high, he pushed all his pain down inside and kept it covered up by playing the game. He had actually become so good at the game that he had forgotten the life he had led without it, the game had completely taken over to the point that he wasn't playing it anymore, but now in fact, the game was playing him.

Navi was completely oblivious to the internal dilemma her driver was experiencing. She could only think of herself right now and the situation she was digging herself deeper and deeper into. It seemed like ever since she started this little journey there have been nothing but roadblocks in the way of her moving forward. Now she certainly had a lot to consider, especially after all she had experienced in just the last 12 hours.

If all she had just been through and all she had just witnessed had truly been real, then what could she say of anything she had believed up until now? Did radios really talk and have minds of their own? Are there really giant, mourning moons that hang sorrowfully over despondent cities that are trapped in patterns of sinful desires and shameful lust? And is there really a giant man who would come to her rescue in a dirty motel room when her life is being choked out by a drug overdose? Is there really a hero who would pursue her in the midst of her guilt and shame only to part the raging waters of a rushing river to carry her to the other side and make her clean?

As these thoughts were swimming through her mind, the driver was aimlessly driving up one avenue and down the next. The night and its darkness were slowly being chased away by a hazy glow. A new day was dawning behind the ratty little houses they were passing by. Every traffic light they would stop at seemed to pulsate with life, like a beating heart. Even as the shady shadows of people would disappear into the alleys and into the shanties, there seemed almost to be a promise in their disappearances. Every breath Navi was breathing seemed to become strangely full of purpose.

The driver had finally gotten enough of a hold on himself to swallow the lump in his throat. Now all he could think of was that he wanted to get rid of this girl. Even with all the money she had brought to him in just a few short hours, this emotional strain just didn't seem worth it. He was prepared to drop her at the bus stop and hoped he would never see her again.

"Gurrrl, I'ma take you down hurr to dis bus station gurrl. You gunna hafta git yerself outta dis cadillac car and find you another pimp gurrrl. I cayn't take dis no more gurrrl," he mumbled as he pulled up along the big glass doors of the old, run-down station. "An take dis money, ho. I cayn't well spend it knowing bout all dat craziness dat just went down back thurr. Take it all," he commanded her as he thrust a huge wad of money at her.

Navi knew that was more than she had brought him and she couldn't understand why he was giving her all this cash, but she scooped up her tattered little backpack and unzipped it, took the wad of bills and stuffed it down inside the bag. She didn't waste any time on goodbyes either, as soon as the money was in her bag she opened the car door and got out. Not a moment after she shut the door and stepped up onto the sidewalk, the pimp sped off in his cadillac.

As she stood here on the threshold of this bus station she suddenly felt very ashamed. The hazy dawn was bringing an odd light around about her and she began to sense her dissidence with her surroundings. Her filthy socks and shoes and muddy legs were exposed with just a little threadbare flap of plaid material hanging around her waist as a skirt and a disheveled, grungy oxford draped loosely over her shoulders, spatters of mud and blood flung across it as well.

That was what Navi saw when she looked down at herself, but what she couldn't see was the giant bruise that all but covered half of her face. Actually, that bruise started at the top of her forehead where her head had been slammed into the dumpster, then grew into a huge brown and green bruise covering the side of her face, from above her eyebrow to below her jaw bone. Her eye was beginning to swell a bit and the entire side of her face was getting tight and sore. That bruise even continued down her neck and shoulder, completely covering that side of her body.

It was obvious to anyone who looked at her that this was evidence that she had been battered and beaten, but Navi didn't think of herself as broken. She saw herself as weak and foolish, she saw herself as lonely and forgotten. She saw herself as less than, as unworthy. Suddenly the feeling of shame was replaced with the emptiness and desperation that accompanies the sense of abandonment. A frantic rush of emotion stirred within her and she started looking all around her at the people passing by, looking down on her with disgust, and she realized there was a total disconnect from them. She was surrounded by people, yet utterly alone. The realization of that separation from those around her was nearly overwhelming.

The haziness of the dawn had transformed into a smattering of points of light that speckled her body. She stood there, nearly naked but flecked with light, with the judgmental glares of the people zooming past her. Again tears began to well up in her eyes. She felt so isolated and forsaken and was so overwhelmed with emotion that inevitably, the tears escaped her eyes and began to run down her cheeks. But, instead of flowing down to her chest, each tear became a ball of light and lifted off her face and floated around about her. Suddenly, she was not isolated but had abruptly been transported to another realm where the superficial people no longer swarmed around her.

The giant man who had rescued her and taken her to the banks of the mighty river was there. He was dressed in shining white garments with a gilded belt around his waist and a purple sash draped across his torso. He stood in the gates, waiting for her. She lifted up her head and stood before the ancient door, beholding the beauty of the glorious King. She saw that he was strong and mighty, mighty in battle and ready to fight for her, ready to fight on her behalf.

Navi came and stood before him and beheld his beauty. He was shining and bright, gloriously transformed before her into a flashing light. She wanted him near her, she wanted to be near him. With her heart pounding in her throat she went forward and leaned into his chest. He smelled like light and life, like the wind blowing across a rolling meadow in the country. As she leaned into him and he wrapped his giant arms around her she felt that he was as strong as he was kind and as gentle as he was brave. She melted into him and allowed herself to completely yield to his embrace. There was nothing unclean or impure about the way he held her and she felt so safe and whole wrapped in his arms. She realized in that moment that being near him was the only place she wanted to be. She had finally found where she belonged, in his presence.

It could have been minutes or it could have been days that Navi was just being held. Time seemed to stop or stretch, she wasn't sure which. But it didn't matter in that moment. The more she pressed into him, it seemed there was more of him to love her. As she lingered, there were layers of his love that were unfolding around her to the point of consuming her. She didn't know that it was happening, but the longer she let him love her, the less she was remaining bruised and battered. It was as if this embrace erased the evidence of abuse and she was being healed and restored.

The other thing that Navi didn't know was that she was drawing strength for the next battle she would face.

Is this the way You show to me?
Do I let go
and let You lead?
Why can't I just let You be
and totally
learn to be free?

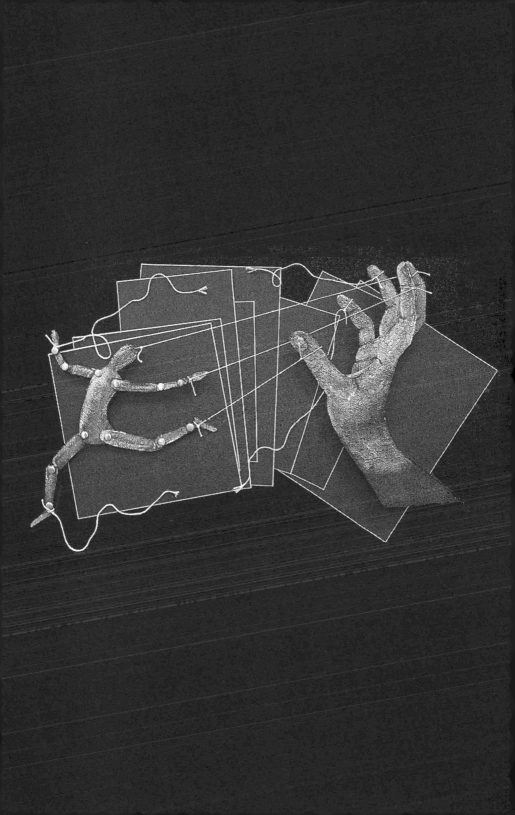

Nine

～

"BLIND AMBITION"

As quickly as Navi was swept up into that safe, lovely place, she was jerked back to the cold, harsh reality of the stoop in front of the bus station. She was yanked from behind as a big, sweaty hand was placed over her face and she was swiftly snatched away into the back of an empty van that had pulled up to the curb. Looking through the gaps between her capturer's big, fat fingers, she saw the world she was being whisked away from swirling out and away from her in broken fragments.

As she was thrust to the floor of the van, her backpack spilled open and all of the money was strewn across the carpet. Navi was terrified as she realized the man who had thrown her down was not the least bit concerned with the money flying everywhere. He had an evil look in his eye and was set on only one thing. She screamed and tried to twist away from him as the driver of the van bolted into traffic.

The evil man's massive, sweaty hands groped at her and grabbed onto her. He manhandled her into submission, grabbing her chest by reaching around her from behind. Pressing her face down into the floor, he squeezed her with one of his hulking arms and the other hand fumbled as he undid the zipper of his pants and jerked her skirt up. Navi was so terrified she involuntarily urinated all over his hand but that didn't stop him from doing the unthinkable. The girl screamed and fought to get away from him, twisting and turning and trying with all she had to fight him off. He just kept pursuing her with his fat, drippy hands and huge bulking body thrown on top of her.

The harder she tried to fight him off, the more he smashed himself against her. They were rolling back and forth on the floor of the van as the driver sped around corners and slammed the brakes to stop at intersections only to punch the gas and speed off, the clumsy vehicle lurching back and forth and side to side as he spun through the city streets.

Navi didn't know who these men were, but she knew they only wanted to hurt her. She was getting so exhausted from the fight she was just grunting little grunts and trying with all the strength she could muster to push the gross, bloated body off of her, but it did no good. She was like an ant trying to flip over a watermelon and eventually her tired arms simply couldn't put up a fight any longer and she gave up, becoming a limp, numb pile of flesh that the disgusting man heaved himself against.

It didn't take him long at all to finish his vicious act and once he had discharged himself, he rolled over and fastened his zipper, wheezing and panting to catch his breath as he laid in the same spot where Navi had peed just minutes before. The girl's stomach lurched as she realized the level at which this man had just violated her and she turned her head to be sick. The raper rolled over onto his hands and knees and then awkwardly made his way up into the passenger seat.

Navi quickly realized the driver wasn't zipping through city streets like a maniac any longer. They now seemed to just be barreling along at a steady, high rate of speed. Navi was afraid of where he might be taking her and what might be happening, but she thought that there could be absolutely nothing worse than the horrible things she had already endured.

Some of the bills that had spilled from her backpack had gotten wet and were stuck to her rear end and her legs. Thinking of what had happened, she felt ashamed to have peed all over the place, but she had been so scared. The fear came back over her like a wave and it all but blinded her, causing her to nearly lose consciousness. As she laid on the wet carpet on the floor in the back of that van, she floated somewhere between cognizance and fainting, from time to time being jostled around by little bumps in the road.

When the driver finally arrived at his destination, the sky was close to showing it's high noon brightness. As he put the smouldering vehicle in park, Navi became keenly aware that they were in a secluded location, far away from the city. She propped herself up on her elbows and looked around, seeing through the windshield only glimpses of leafy tree branches being fluttered by the wind. The passenger turned his body in his seat and put his feet and legs to the center console, so he was facing the driver at the side angle. What Navi saw next caused her to sit straight up, and she almost even let out a squeal.

The wicked man was holding two of her most desired items - a glass pipe in one hand and a torch lighter in the other. As he took a long hit from the pipe, Navi instantly smelled the aroma of the crack cocaine wafting into the back of the van and mixing with the pungent odors of vomit, urine and sweat. She wanted that pipe so badly she could cry.

He passed it to the driver who took his turn inhaling the thick, white smoke and then passed it back to his counterpart. Once the glass cooled off, the man took a pencil-like rod and slowly pushed the brillo filter to the opposite end of the pipe. Navi knew what he was doing; this was an unclean, dirty hit, but it was necessary to burn away the thick layer of oil that had settled on the back side of the filter after smoking thru only one end. What happened next surprised her.

The man turned completely around in his seat and saw her sitting up in the back of the van, watching him and the driver smoke. He motioned to her almost as if he was asking her if she wanted some as well. Navi nodded her head up and down quickly, keeping her round eyes fixed on that pipe. The man rolled out of his seat and crawled back to where she was, then put the pipe to her lips and lit it up so she could take that dirty hit.

To the desperate girl, even the dirty, leftover scum on the end of the used filter was more than she'd had for so long, and the dope was so potent it sent her reeling backwards. As she exhaled a billowing cloud of smoke, her ears started ringing shrilly and Navi nearly went blind.

She laid back on the damp carpet and her entire body was twitching and convulsing as the drugs coursed through her veins. This was the place she had desired to get to for so long, and she was so wrecked now that she wouldn't be able to turn away even if she wanted to.

The driver came and sat with them at the back of the van and they started a little ritual there. The man with the fat fingers would pack a piece of dope on the pipe and smoke it. Then, he would hand it over to the driver, who would do the same and hand it right back to the fat-fingered man. Once the pipe cooled, he would push the filter and hold the pipe up to Navi's lips, allowing her to partake in the dirty, nearly wasted hit. She didn't complain one bit at all. As far as she was concerned, this was better than nothing.

After a few times of the circle of smoking cycled through, when the driver took his hit, he leaned toward Navi and pressed his lips to hers. Then he blew smoke from his mouth directly into hers. While he did this he put his hand on her knee and slid it all the way up the inside of her thigh as she leaned in to inhale the hit. Navi held that smoke in her lungs until Mr. Fatfingers prepared the pipe for her again, then she took that hit as he held the pipe to her lips. This little routine went on for quite a while, but every time the man passed onto her the hit he exhaled, he was more brazen with where he put his fingers and hands on her body and with each turn Navi was more open and accommodating to his fondlings.

They stayed in the back of that van and just kept smoking for hours. The time slipped by like nothing and they didn't converse at all. They just let out little awkward grunts and cleared their throats or coughed from time to time. And the longer this went on, the crazier the looks flickering through the two men's eyes became. After some time, the little sticky white piles of dope were nearly gone and Navi could barely see straight from all the smoking. Her head was spinning and her body was pulsating that whomp-whomp-whomp that she remembered from what seemed so long ago.

As the daylight shining between the tree branches dancing in front of the windshield began to fade and take on a softer, golden glow, Navi couldn't stand it anymore. The touching, the smoking, the whomp-whomp-whomp just sent her over the deep end. As the hit she was pulling from the pipe filling up her tiny lungs, she leaned back a little too far and smashed the back of her head on the dirty floor of the van.

At once, she was out like a light. She floated away from herself and into a realm of total darkness. But, this darkness was quite different than the evil, demonic darkness that she experienced with her eyes open, walking the streets in her living-hell reality. This darkness was more like a warm, quiet place where everything was still and completely at peace. And it wasn't darkness as is experienced from a lack of light or by an emptiness, but it almost seemed to be a region where anything, including light, was prohibited from escaping. As if this place was absorbing all the light that hit the horizon, yet reflecting nothing. Completely filled to the uttermost.

As she found herself in the total darkness, she felt the warm, moist breath of her enormous friend and champion brushing across her face as he whispered in her ear, "Hello, Navi."

Then she said to herself, "Oh, He even sees me in the dark! At night I'm immersed in His light!"

She realized he made darkness his canopy around himself, and she so needed him there with her. She drew close to him, hoping he would draw near to her, and he certainly did not disappoint! She felt him cover her with his massive, loving arms and hold her in such a tight hug that her body could have just melted away like butter left on a sunny windowsill. She allowed herself to fully submit to his embrace and completely gave herself over to him.

"Navi, you are one of my children of light. You are a daughter of the day, not created of night, nor owned by darkness. My child, I want you to walk in the light as I am in the light, so we can be together and I can purify you from all of these sins being committed against you."

The girl nuzzled down deeper into the always-unfolding layers of his love that she found herself wrapped in. It seemed that as she pressed herself into him more, he expanded. As if the more of him she acquainted herself with, the more of him there was to find and to know. She found herself tunneled deep into the cocoon that he had become, as safe as she could be, in the deepest place she could trust herself to go. As odd as it seemed, she felt like she was in his womb. There, in that place of total darkness, wrapped in the never ending layers of this man, buried down deep inside of him - in that place - she found a light that was shining brighter than the noonday sun.

Navi let that bright light envelop and pervade her. She became absolutely consumed by the light as it saturated her and began radiating all of her surroundings. The light wasn't exposing her, but revealing her as she unfolded a million times and blossomed forth from the womb she had hidden in. Now, standing in the blinding light with everything around her glowing and blazing as well, she felt for the first time in her life as if she were truly alive.

Ten

~

"BEGGING FOR MERCY"

I n the stark reality of the smelly floor in the back of the raggedy van, Navi began to come to. It started with the smells, that stench of urine and vomit and crack smoke that was so pungent and clinging to the air in the small space. Then, she felt her sense of touch returning a little at a time. She could feel tingling in her hands and legs, she could feel the pressure of a large object pressing down on her, she could feel the warm, wet sensation close to her ear, but she wasn't exactly sure what that was. She could feel the wind blowing against her skin and felt as though she were swaying up and down and side-to-side. As her hearing returned she could hear a low grunting and the squeaking of metal springs being compressed and released. Her sight returned a bit at a time and she started putting these things all together. Even in the dim lighting she could see the sweaty man on top of her, his eyes clenched and his big, fat lips puffing out little blasts of breath and low grunts.

Before she fully knew what was happening, he got up and turned away from her, climbing out the open sliding door of the van. As he walked away, buckling his pants up, another young dark-skinned man wearing a beanie hat climbed in the van and mounted himself on top of her. He grabbed ahold of the hair on top of her head, tangled his hands up in it and quickly started thrusting himself on her like a dog humping somebody's leg.

Navi just laid there, completely still and unable to move even a muscle. She was still quite high from all the smoking and that whomp-whomp-whomp sensation was still fading in and out. She was terrified by what was happening to her, but there was no way she could put up a fight so she opted to just lay there.

As the man in the hat got up and crawled out the doorway, another very young man climbed in. This one was maybe only 17 years old and he almost looked as scared as Navi felt. He kept his eyes closed and just laid on top of her, moving his hips up and down a little bit until he finished and rolled over, climbing out through the open door.

Navi lost count of how many men came through the door of that van. Some of them just laid on top of her, some of them lifted up her hips and legs, some of them pulled her hair and slapped her face, one of them spat on her. She knew there were a lot of men and that they were all standing under the trees outside because she could hear them drinking and laughing and yelling back and forth to one another over the loud rap music playing from a car radio. She could also smell the odor of marijuana blunts wafting into the back of the van, so she knew they were all out there partying and having a good ol' time. She just figured she must be the main attraction of their party.

Right about the time when Navi had nearly come to the point of accepting what was happening to her, a lanky dark skinned man climbed up in the back of the van and said, "Damn, you smell like an old, worn-out boot."

That was all it took to send her over the edge and back into reality, and she felt big, hot tears welling up in her eyes. As he climbed on top of her, she turned her face and heaved a puddle of vomit on the floor next to her head, right where he had just placed his hand.

He started yelling crude obscenities at her and used the hand that she had thrown up on to backhand her across her face. She just laid there and stared him in the eyes, looking at a man who had purely evil motives. He wasn't intimidated or ashamed of her staring at him, either; he held her gaze like a snake and kept pounding himself on top of her.

Navi started to see that same seeping, oozing blackness that had wrapped itself around her in her hotel room making its way across the face of this man. Before she knew it, he was completely covered and consumed by the blackness and all she could see besides the inky shape of his face and body were the glowing coal embers of his eyes.

As he pounded himself harder and harder against her, Navi held her breath. She didn't want to receive the darkness into herself like she had in the hotel room. She just resisted it and resisted it. She actually started thinking about the experience she had just been through where the darkness became light. She closed her eyes and saw the loving and always kind face of her champion-king who had held her so deeply and so sweetly. With her eyes shut and picturing his beautiful face, it was almost as if she was there with him again. "I want to be under YOU," Navi said to him in her mind.

Somehow, with that confession made in her mind, a power was released outside of her own head. The darkness evaporated and the man who had been so consumed by it suddenly looked to be full of fear. His face drained of its color and his mouth fell open in terror. He pulled himself up, dismounted her and started slinking away from her, crawling backwards on his knees with his hands held up in front of his face and his head turned down and to the side. He started crying out for help, but the clamor of music was so loud no one outside of the van could hear him.

Navi propped herself up on her elbows and turned her head to look over her shoulder. She just had to see what it was that had scared him so much. What she saw surprised her - a humongous, magnificent lion stood behind her, his mane glowing of golden light. The lion's face was huge; each of his eyes was larger than a grown man's fist and his mouth spread more than a foot wide.

The enormous lion had stepped forward and shifted all his weight to his massive front paws. He nearly filled the back of the van and weighed close to half a ton. The man was wailing and shaking, terrified at the beast who now stood over the girl, but the lion seemed more intent on protecting Navi than he did on attacking the man. The man trembled, all the while begging for mercy, as he slipped away through the van's open side door.

As soon as he made it to the crowd and started screaming about what he had seen, there were suddenly sounds of doors slamming and engines starting, gravel spinning and cars speeding off.

It seemed they were all alone in the back of the van and Navi took that opportunity to get closer to the lion. She buried her face in his radiant mane and nuzzled him, breathing in his rich, musky fragrance and being filled with peace. She felt so close to him, so close to her purpose and destiny. She felt redemption drawing near and the joy of knowing that she had been saved started bubbling up inside of her.

Navi and the lion laid down together and her body and mind finally felt totally at rest. Snuggled up against the gigantic beast, she was safer than she had ever been before. The lion made a barrier round about her, using his body and tail to encircle her.

In that warm lion-cocoon she rested and healed, supernaturally being restored with every deep breath entering her lungs. Though she had been naked, she felt garments of white covering her as she laid with the lion.

After a while, sounds invaded the van and Navi was keenly aware a vehicle was pulling up to the deserted road the van was parked on. As she sat up and gained her bearings, she realized in a flash the lion was gone. There was no time for her to wonder where he had gone. Suddenly, there were headlights shining into the van and then crunching gravel underfoot as a man walked up to the open door, his huge silhouette casting a shadow over her.

"Navi, come with me." said the man who stood before her.

Even without being able to see his facial features or anything that would identify him, Navi knew for certain this man was the police officer she had seen in the hotel room the day that the evil blackness had tried to overtake her; the same man who had picked her up when she was on the street corner and taken her to the banks of the mighty river.

She crawled out of the van door and wrapped her arms around his waist. He returned the gesture by scooping her up in his massive arms.

"Come with me, child," he whispered to her.

Navi let the man carry her to his waiting car and sat her down carefully in the passenger seat. He went around the front of the car and took his place at the steering wheel, quickly backing up and leaving the raggedy van behind them as he sped off.

They made their way down the twisting and turning back roads in silence, and before long they were merging onto the Interstate, adding themselves to the sparse count of vehicles on the highway in the middle of nowhere at that late hour of the night. Navi felt so peaceful and rested and in that sweet silence she found herself thinking about how lovely it had been for the lion to heal her and clean her and dress her in white.

Eleven

~

"ALONG THE WAY"

As the car meandered down the highway, weaving its
way in and out, around the occasional semi truck or
sedan, there were so many questions Navi wanted to ask.
As the thoughts would come to the front of her mind, the
moment she would begin to ponder them it seemed as if
a still, small voice in her heart would flood her with peace.

The questions that popped into her mind ranged
from curiosity about how the man knew she was in that
van deep in the backwoods, to why had it taken so long
for him to arrive. Each thought would swim through her
mind and then fade. She would feel anxiety welling up
inside as she considered the question but then that warm
sense of peace would overwhelm her and chase away the
concerns like a felt eraser passing over a chalkboard.

Navi knew they were headed west and started seeing the signs along the interstate informing them that the city was getting closer. When she thought of all the depravity and defilement she had experienced in that city she would start to feel distressed again, but it seemed like any thoughts of fear would quickly pass. It was as if they just simply melted away.

"Navi," said the driver in his deep, rich voice, "My perfect love drives out fear. You can't be afraid when you're in my presence. Any thoughts of concern will fade when I am near. I am the Person of Love, completely made, designed and purposed to give you the example of love alive. I am here to allow you access to my Father, who rules the Kingdom of Love forever."

Navi looked at the profile of the man as he fixed his eyes straight ahead, watching the road as he drove down the highway. She knew that each word he spoke was the absolute and ultimate truth. There was something inside of her that would come alive with his every word, like a heartbeat she had never felt before. He released so much life and peace as he spoke and she was gaining confidence with each syllable. Each word he spoke carried the full weight of its meaning.

The girl felt so much weight lift from her. It seemed as if every cruel act that had ever been committed against her faded into darkness and she could see a vision of herself the way she had been created and designed to be. This version of Navi didn't have any of the damage that she had felt throughout her life, this Navi was whole and complete.

It was such a stark contrast and the more she would press into the vision of herself whole, the more she longed to be restored. It was as if she had been awakened to the purpose she had been created for. Navi just wanted to hear him speak over her more and more.

She scooted over in the seat and put her head on his lap as he drove. The beautiful white dress draped across her and the hem fluttered down into a little pile on the passenger side floorboard. Navi felt so clean and whole.

As she listened to the hum of the tires on the road, she closed her eyes but could still sense the faintest beginnings of light starting to glow outside of the car. She knew the sun would be coming up soon and she really had no desire to see the sinful city they were getting ever closer to. Navi sighed a big sigh and asked the man, "Will you tell me your story?"

Her companion laughed a lovely laugh and said, "I would love to, Navi." He laughed his little laugh again and started telling her a magnificent story that began on the other edge of eternity.

As Navi snuggled her head down in his lap, he wove a glorious tale of working with his father to hang the stars in an empty sky and form each of the planets and creatures with just a word. His voice lit up when he shared about the day they decided to mold a man out of the clay. When he told her about blowing his breath into the clay-man's nostrils, he spoke of the breath itself as if it were a person who had been with he and his father from before the beginning.

The man told her about fashioning a mate for his breathing clay-man by taking part of the clay-man and adding part of himself to make a new creature who was just like Navi, a clay-woman with spirit-breath in her lungs.

He talked for a long time about the clay couple and it was quite obvious that he really loves them. They spent time together everyday for many, many years, until one day, a tragedy happened. The clay couple had been tricked by a slimy, oozy, black creature - just like the one Navi had experienced - and he had convinced them that they didn't want to visit with the man or his father anymore.

Something interesting had happened when they allowed themselves to believe the black creature. At that instant the spirit-breath came out of them and all that was left inside of the clay people was plain old air and a faint memory of what it had been like to have the spirit-breath. They quickly became ashamed and embarrassed and all they wanted to do was to hide from the man and his father.

This absolutely broke the man's heart and he and his father and the spirit-breath knew that in order to share the love that they had with the clay people they had to initiate a plan. So, from that moment forth, every single second of creation would be used to bring the relationship back between the father, son and spirit and the people of clay.

The man told Navi all about the clay-people's journey and how they had set out to start a family. From their own bodies they brought forth clay children that looked just like themselves. It was truly a glorious story, but every bit was mixed with just a touch of sadness because although the clay people grew and multiplied and inhabited the earth, no matter what each of their lives was like, there was always the bitter ending of death.

Even with the tinges of sorrow, the lives he spoke about were each so magnificent. There were amazing stories of nations and kingdoms, journeys through wilderness and victory over enemies. It was as if the story he told her, his story, was about each and every single person who had ever lived or was yet to live upon the earth. And the man even spoke of angels too! He knew each of their names and their individual characteristics and traits.

Navi's heart burned inside of her chest as he recited to her the lists of laws and customs that all of society has been based upon and spoke to her of a peculiar people who wanted to come to him instead of hide from him. She knew by the aching inside of herself that those laws were what this man was made of and the peculiar people was the family she belonged in.

The story continued as he spoke passionately of a plan he had worked out with his father and the spirit, a plan laid out before they even started hanging the stars in the empty sky. The plan involved this man leaving the place where he spent every bit of his time with his father and the spirit-breath. Instead he would actually come to earth and be one of the clay people so he could share his love with them all. The plan worked out even though the clay people rejected him and ended up killing him.

The man spoke about the day he had died so matter-of-factly that Navi didn't even question the validity. It was the ultimate fulfillment of destiny for him to die, and as Navi quickly realized, he didn't stay in the world of death but he rose again to life! This mystery was so hard to believe but at the same time, it made so much sense. Navi absolutely, without a shadow of a doubt, knew the man had died, but now he was certainly alive!

It seemed like he had talked for days or months or years but, in reality, the man had told Navi the story of all of creation up until this point in just a matter of about an hour. He ran his massive hand along her forehead and said, "My child, we have arrived."

Navi sat up in the seat and peered out the windshield and was surprised to see that they had already crossed through the city and were now on the other side of the river. The man had parked in the middle of an empty field and the car was pointed back towards the city skyline with the beautiful bridge and giant pyramid on the other side of the river, directly in the middle of their line of vision.

"Come with me, Navi," said the man as he exited the car. He walked around to open her door and stood there expectantly, his hand outstretched towards her and a huge grin spread across his face.

Navi took his hand and slid out of the car, her beautiful white gown shimmering in the pink-and-purple haze of the almost-sunrise. He led her to the bank of the river and they could look across to the pyramid on the other side. He stood before her, his big, broad shoulders and body blocking out the pyramid from her view. As the sun climbed up in the sky and seemed to rise above his head, a huge set of glorious wings spread out from his back and he raised his hands up at his sides.

In an instant she saw the man for who he truly was. He was the man who had come to her room and comforted her every night of her childhood after those bad men had done those bad things to her. He was the man who protected her when two years ago, at just 12 years old, she had decided to run away from the house where she had lived with the man who had given her the fruity drinks and made movies of her with his friends every night. This was the man who came and slept beside her when she slept under the bridge just around the corner from her house.

This man was the man who had loved her and protected her her entire life! Navi knew he truly had conquered over death, because until this moment she had wanted to die, but now, standing in the shadow of his beautiful wings, she wanted to live life fully alive.

Twelve

~

"Twist of Fate"

Navi was in awe of the beauty of the man. She became fully aware of who he was and who she was in him. She knew in an instant that he was, in fact, the father, and himself the son, and the spirit-breath all at once. He looked down at her with his fiery eyes of love and she could see her entire destiny playing out inside of them.

Overwhelmed by his love and overtaken with passion and purpose, Navi fell to her knees in total worship. She began to cry big, hot tears upon the tops of the man's giant bare feet and she wiped them with her long locks of hair. With each tear running down the sides of his massive feet and each stroke of her hair she fell more and more in love, kissing his feet and hugging his ankles.

The more her tears gushed, the more she poured out her love upon him. His feet were the most beautiful thing her eyes had ever seen. She wanted to kiss them forever. But as she wept, he bent down and picked her up and held her to himself.

As he held her close to his chest, his wings wrapped across in front of himself and made a little tent that hid them from the outside. Inside of the wing-tent Navi marveled as the man gazed upon her with those loving fire-eyes. Every color imaginable was pulsating forth from his face and they were surrounded by such a fantastic light that it seemed to even have a life itself! The wing-tent was the most beautiful and serene place Navi had ever even dreamed of and she wanted to stay there forever.

Navi stayed buried in the flashing-rainbow-light wing-tent for what seemed like eons. She fell more and more in love with the man with each flash of light and every flicker of his fire-eyes. Layer upon layer of love unfolded and consumed her, swallowing her up and taking her into a still deeper and greater revelation of love.

After what seemed like days and months and years, the wing-tent unfurled and Navi was again exposed to the elements of the outside world, but she was not affected by them the same way now. She had experienced such love that she had been transformed. Her heart had come to life and that slightly familiar place where she had been lacking in the spirit-breath was now filled to overflowing with both breath and spirit.

The man let Navi down and she stood before him, spotless and radiant, reflecting back at him the glory of himself, her beloved. It seemed impossible that she could contain any more love, but as she stood there and they beheld one another, her heart was being filled again and again with more, and more, and more, love, and love, and love.

"This is the one and only thing that I want to do forever," said Navi. "I want to gaze at your beauty and live inside of that wing-tent with you every day of my life!"

"Ha ha, Navi!" he laughed. "You've got it, girl! That's the best thing you could ever seek or desire!

'Navi, this is what you were created for. I made you for love. And although I know that nothing would ever make you happier than to stay in this place forever, I brought you here for a very special reason. In the same way that you have received this love from me, I am going to send you - filled with my love and filled with the breath of my spirit - to take this love into the world and find hurting and broken people to share it with. Deposit my love into them, Navi, and watch as the world around you becomes transformed by love.

'I have overcome the darkness, and in me there is only light. I have overcome death, and in me there is life everlasting. I have overcome the grave, and in me there is a place of rebirth and restoration. I am the key to destiny, Navi. Share me with all those you encounter, anyone who has been afflicted and affected by sin, everyone who fears the end of this life and each person who feels lost and alone.

'This is how you will keep the fire of my love burning in your heart, by sharing my love freely. Tell them the story I shared with you along the way and they will see themselves in it, just as you saw yourself in my story, Navi. This is the secret to life everlasting: deposit my gift of love to grow in the lives of my people and release them into the promise and destiny for which I created them."

Navi was once again moved by the enormity of this love. She hung on each syllable that was being spoken over her and could feel the full weight of meaning unfolding from every single word he declared. She was being stretched to the point of breaking but was still able to contain all that he was pouring into her.

"Navi, because you are filled with my love and the breath of my spirit, you'll be able to overcome every obstacle that is ever set before you. You will see, in fact, that the obstacles are actually a way for you to receive an even greater portion of my love.

'I am sending you now, as my daughter. You will see many set free and transformed by my love. Let my spirit within you lead you along the way and always remember the story I shared with you. So long as you continue to be filled with this love, you will never, ever fail. My love for you is never-ending, Navi."

Navi again knelt on the ground before the man, but this time instead of crying on his feet she actually laid flat upon the ground, face-down at his feet. She laid there for quite some time, just soaking in the ripples and waves of love.

After a while had passed, Navi lifted her head and she saw the most beautiful sight - the sun perched atop the apex of the pyramid across the river. It was as if the sunrise had stopped and the ages she had spent with her beautiful savior had taken no time at all from the physical world.

Navi stood up and saw that the beautiful, glowing white gown she had been wearing had been transformed into a military-style outfit that was something like an iridescent swat team uniform. She knew that now she was on a mission and she had a purpose and a destiny before her. With a grateful heart she stood up and began to walk toward the western sky, her back turned to the Egypt of her past and her face turned to her future of freedom.

About the Artist

~

A lexis Kadonsky is a fine artist, 3D animator, and designer from Chicagoland, born in 1990.

On a fully funded art scholarship, Alexis received a BFA in graphic design from the University of Illinois Ubana-Champaign. She continues on to achieve her MFA in 3D Computer Animation from the School of Visual Arts in New York City and was named Sony Pictures Imageworks IPAX Scoredos Scholar for exemplary achievements and truly special talent and passion for film, effects, and animation.

Alexis embraces her attention to detail throughout many mediums as demonstrated in her diverse portfolio. Art acts as an escape for Alexis, and she strives to tell a unique story with her work while enjoying getting lost in the process of creating. She also has a passion for travel and has spent about two years of her life traveling around Europe and Australia to further expand her views on art and the world. Although her work is inspired from many paths, Alexis believes her best creativity ignites from her personal experiences.

See more of Alexis Kadonsky's work at www.alexiska-donsky.com.

About the Cover

~

When I sat down with Alexis to discuss the cover art for Hello Navi, I had already explored her portfolio and knew without a shadow of a doubt she was the right person to create this image. During our meeting, ideas and thoughts that had been running through my head flowed out quickly, and she listened attentively, taking notes and asking many questions.

More than anything, I wanted to somehow display the face of the heroine of our story: a broken young lady who was for the first time in her life experiencing love. I saw in my mind a young lady who had been heading in one direction, and she suddenly hears a booming voice call out to her, "Hello, Navi!" As Navi turns to see who is calling her by name, the light starts shining on a face that has been in darkness for too long. I could see her wild hair swirling all around her head as she looked over her shoulder, an expression of curiosity, wonder and intrigue somehow apparent on her face.

Alexis produced an image that was far beyond the ideas that I had in my head, and I knew it was absolutely perfect for this book. She created a beautiful face of a young lady who can not be defined as any specific ethnicity, but instead incorporates features of every race. Although she has witnessed many atrocities and experienced great trauma, simply turning toward the radiance of the Light of the World, she is instantly being renewed and healed. The curiosity in her eyes is evident and the light falling across her is transforming her from darkness to a child of light.

The name Navi is actually Hebrew for "prophet" which can be defined as a spokesperson of some doctrine, cause, or movement. Little Navi was brought out of the life of commercial sex trade and she grew up to be Sandy Storm, an author and abolitionist who unashamedly proclaims the doctrine of her Lord Jesus Christ, who she is head-over-heels in love with.

My life has been transformed from victim to survivor, and now I am truly thriving.

"For you were once darkness, but now you are light in the Lord. Walk as children of light"

EPHESIANS 5:8 NKJV